HEAD ROCK HARBOR MYSTERY #3

PRIDE
AND
PUNCTURE

CHASE CONNOR

Book Cover Designed By:
©2025 Chase Connor; Chase Connor Books

Published By:

Chase Connor Books
www.chaseconnor.com

AUTHORS' NOTE:
This is a work of fiction. Names, characters, places, and incidents either are the product of the authors' imagination or are used fictitiously, and any resemblance to actual persons, living or dead, business establishments, events, or locales is entirely coincidental. None of this is real.

E-book ISBN 978-1-951860-51-6
Paperback ISBN 978-1-951860-52-3

Table of Contents

HEAD ROCK HARBOR
PRIDE

Day 1
Friday, June 7th

6 p.m. Harbor Street - Parade of Rainbows
7 p.m. Town Square - Pride Feast*
9p.m. Harbor Street - The Rainbow Lights**

Day 2
Saturday, June 8th

12 p.m. The Harbor - Pride Picnic - BYOPB
2 p.m. The Sandbar - Swimming & Live Music
4 p.m. Harbor Street - Tour the shops of Harbor Street
6 p.m. The Dock - Pride Food & Wine Pairings***
9 p.m. Harper's Bar & Grill - Rainbow Rave****

Day 3
Sunday, June 9th

11 a.m. The Dock - Pride Brunch w/ Bottomless Mimosas
3 p.m. Head Rock Harbor P.D. Parking Lot - Tolerance Conference*****
5 p.m. Town Square - Pride BBQ******
7 p.m. Head Rock Harbor Books - Meet the LGBTQ Author - Taylor C. Tomlin*******
9 p.m. The Harbor - Rainbow Fireworks Display - BYOB

*Local eateries will be providing food at low cost to all. $5 per plate per person.
**Harbor Street will be lit up like a rainbow! Will be lit every night of Pride weekend!
***21+ only event; ticket event. Tickets can be purchased at the hostess podium at The Dock or by using their website. SOLD OUT.
****18+ only event. Entry fee required. Talk to Deb Harper for details.
*****Chief Marvin Bucksworth and Mayor Linda Wagner will be giving speeches and education on tolerance.
******All BBQ, sides, and drinks are free to all – provided by Head Rock Harbor Town Council, cooked by Beau and Sawyer Robison, and Lardell Simmons. Will be filling plates until food runs out.
*******18+ only event; ticket event. Light refreshments will be available. Tickets can be purchased at Head Rock Harbor Books. SOLD OUT.

Chapter One

Considering all of the excitement in town, you'd think that the citizens of Head Rock Harbor had never attended a special event of any kind in their lives. For weeks people had been stopping by to simply stare at the calendar of events posted in the front windows of all of the shops on Harbor Street. Pride was still six days away, but every day had already been a parade up and down the street, consisting of excited townsfolk and curious tourists.

After a harried month of planning—during which time I still had to run a business, meet my writing deadlines, take care of my household, have a personal life, and take care of the furball who held me hostage in my own home—I'd meticulously planned the First Annual Head Rock Harbor Pride Week. Well…week*end*, really. Unofficially, we were calling it "Pride Weekend." Mayor Linda Wagner was thrilled. The business owners in town were excited at the prospect of a weekend sales boom. Townsfolk were excited for all of the fun activities planned—family friendly and otherwise.

Though I felt I could have done better, even for the inaugural Head Rock Harbor Pride, I knew I'd done well enough with the time and budget given. The budget had been small and I'd had barely a month and a half to plan, but I was still satisfied. A solid three-day weekend of festivities was planned for the first Friday through Sunday of June. Daytime events were for families, but after dark, there were plenty of adults-only activities.

As Pride should be.

Especially in a small town like Head Rock Harbor.

When there was only three weeks left until Pride, I'd given all of the businesses on Harbor Street signage for their storefront windows. It was easier to post the list of activities than to have people asking questions every minute of every day.

It wasn't the most exciting Pride Weekend calendar I'd ever seen, but I felt it was impressive for our tiny little town. Though I'd been cautious at first, I found that almost everyone in town—especially the business owners—were excited to be included. As I spent the last part of April and most of May planning the event, I found I didn't lack for helping hands.

Being completely honest with myself, I knew that I couldn't have done better unless the budget had been doubled and I'd had an extra year to organize. Regardless of how things played out, Head Rock Harbor's first annual Pride Weekend was planned. Most importantly—and surprisingly—no one had complained about Pride coming to our little town. That was the thing I happened to be most proud of, though I had no power over other's thoughts and feelings.

As I was leaving the shop, I grabbed the final remaining sign of events and tucked it under my arm. Rattlesnatches gave me the cold shoulder as I shut down the register and stowed my laptop under the check-out counter. He'd been feeling neglected for at least a month, but it was nothing I could help. Being Saturday night, I was closing up shop a few minutes early. I needed to get to Harper's, but for reasons other than to provide my mother the sign to put in her window.

Though I wasn't entirely certain why, I'd been avoiding the date I'd promised Deacon Davis for helping me figure out the cause of death for Carter Nelson. Having to organize the Pride Weekend in such a short amount of time had been my go-to excuse. And it hadn't actually been a total lie. Organizing an entire Pride celebration—even for a small town like Head Rock Harbor—was a Herculean task.

Regardless, Deacon's texts could not be brushed off forever. He was a tenacious little guy. Actually, he'd grown on me over the last month-and-a-half of texts—which had begun as irksome, but grew to be charming. I wanted to be bothered by how insistent he was, but I eventually came to enjoy—and even look forward to—his playful texts.

In the back of my mind, as always, there was Jeremy. The kiss he'd given me in his car after we'd solved Carter Nelson's not-really-murder was like a piece of corn kernel stuck between two molars. Irritating, but so satisfying to pick at all day.

What did it mean?

Was my friend wanting a real relationship for once?

Was I convenient?

A conquest?

A box to check?

How long had he wanted to kiss me?

Shaking my head clear of thoughts, I exited the bookstore, shutting off the lights and locking the door tightly on my way out. As I strode away, Rattlesnatches leapt into the window and scowled at me bitterly. I shot him an apologetic glance as I dashed down Harbor Street, mentally making a note to spend quality time with him soon.

I didn't have time to think about what the kiss from Jeremy truly meant, or what, if anything, I was going to do about it. Besides, in the nearly two months since our shared kiss, he'd kept a noticeable distance. Jeremy hadn't exactly avoided me, but it was obvious that he wasn't making an effort to hang out like we used to do. We'd only had lunch together a handful of times in a month and a half and he never came over for dinner anymore.

The fact that I'd told him I had to think about the kiss had probably bruised his ego. For a guy like Jeremy—who could, and did, get every guy he wanted—my reticence had probably stung. It wasn't that I wasn't attracted to Jeremy— any red-blooded human attracted to men would be. And it wasn't that I thought it was entirely crazy for us to further our relationship. I simply didn't know if I could trust Jeremy's intentions.

He'd been a playboy for so long, I didn't want to end up another notch on his bedpost.

Maybe that was slut shaming my friend, but it was what it was. Jeremy had a new crush every day of the week. If our friendship was going to survive, I couldn't be the soup du jour. Protecting my heart was more important than being politically correct.

I grumbled at myself for continuing to think about Jeremy as I walked towards Harper's. It was the last thing I needed to concern myself with leading up to Pride Weekend. There was still so much to do. Besides, I was about to meet Deacon for drinks at my mother's restaurant. Thinking about a guy while out on a date with another guy showed a complete lack of propriety.

Once I reached Harper's, I'd barely chased the thoughts of Jeremy from my head. I was opening the door to the brightly lit and raucously loud bar and grill when the last nugget of Jeremy fluttered from my brain.

Harper's Bar, Grill, Bait & Tackle, an establishment owned by my mother, Deb Harper, was one of two places the citizens of Head Rock Harbor could get a drink any night of the week. Though Harper's was known to be less shady than Bernie's Tavern on a weekend night, it could still get wild at times. Fortunately, at seven o'clock on a Saturday, dinner service wasn't yet winding down, so the bar had not filled up and gotten too wild yet.

It only took me a moment to spot Deacon. He'd taken up the barstool at the far end of the bar by the jukebox—not the best place to have a drink and conversation. I was going to give him a pass. Maybe he had sat there because it was the only stool empty when he'd arrived. I gave him a wave and indicated to give me a minute.

Deb, my mother, was behind the bar, pouring a Pabst from the tap for Lukey Harlsbad. I wanted to pass the calendar of events off to her before I forgot, or it got crumpled. Side-stepping between two barstools and bellying up to the bar, I held the laminated calendar out to her over the bar. Deb cocked an eyebrow at me as if to say, '*I'm working here, kid.'* I rolled my eyes and let her finish pouring the beer. When she passed the mug off to Lukey, he gave her a thanks and me a nod, then stepped away from the bar to join his friends at a table on the other side of the room.

"You ain't got any patience?" Deb asked, putting her hands on her hips.

"You're the one who has been whining about getting a copy of the calendar for fifteen business days," I replied, jiggling the calendar at her.

With a roll of her eyes, Deb took the calendar from me, gave it a quick glance, and stowed it under the bar.

"I'll have it in the front window before we close up tonight," she said.

"Good," I said. "Harper's is hosting one of the events, after all."

"You want your regular?" she asked, reaching for her pad in her apron. "Go find a seat and—"

"No," I waved her off, pushing away from the bar. "I'm here to meet Deacon."

Confusion swept over Deb's face and her brow furrowed. Her head turned to glance at Deacon, slight and hunched on his barstool. His white-blond hair was swooped to the left side of his head, blocking our view of his face.

"Oh, cheese and rice, Jackson." Deb groaned. "Leave the kid alone."

"Pardon me?" I huffed.

"He's a baby. Too young for you."

"*He's twenty-four.*"

"You're pushing thirty."

"I'm *twenty-seven*," I scowled.

She didn't say anything, but simply shook her head.

"We went to high school together," I added. "Well, for one year. And *he* asked *me* out."

"Well, yeah," Deb put her hands on the bar to brace herself. "Kids are dumb."

I couldn't help it. A laugh rolled from my throat. Deb smiled, unable to ignore the humor of our conversation.

"He's not a kid," I said once I had control of myself. "He's my age. Don't be weird."

"Fine." She waved me off. "You *young men* going to eat or what?"

I shrugged. "I only agreed to drinks."

"You barely drink."

"I barely do anything," I said. "Including going on dates. So don't act a fool and ruin this night for me, if you please."

Deb waggled her head at me and moved her mouth as if mocking me, but no sound passed her lips.

Instead of giving her the satisfaction of a retort, I pushed away from the bar and slid between the stools. Making my way down to the other end of the bar, I slid onto the stool next to Deacon. Right before I'd sat down, someone had chosen to play *Take Me, Home Country Roads* by John Denver. The opening chords of the song began as my rear end connected with wood and the bar erupted with the hoots of appreciative, drunken country music lovers.

Deacon turned to me and pushed his wave of hair to the other side of his head, grimacing. The sides of his head were buzzed, leaving me with a clear view of his face. I laughed and held my hands up in a '*what can you do*' way as numerous people in the bar joined John Denver in singing about West Virginia.

"*Maybe this wasn't the best place to sit?*" Deacon talk-shouted over the noise.

"*I could have told you that.*" I shouted back.

"*Do you want—*" Deacon began.

"*What are you boys drinking?*" I jumped as Deb appeared on the other side of the bar.

Glaring at my mother for a second, I took a moment to glance at Deacon's mug on the bar before him. He'd gone with a beer, so I decided to follow suit.

"*Just give me a Blue Moon!*" I hollered over the growing noise.

She nodded, then looked at Deacon. "*You need a fill up?*" Deacon nodded. "*Sure!*"

Deb gave us a nod and practically glided over to the row of taps to get us our beers. Out of the corner of my eye, I could see Deb watching us closely as she began filling the first mug from the Blue Moon tap. Deciding to ignore her, I turned back to Deacon. However, as soon as I opened my mouth to say something, the noise in the bar swelled and I cringed, swallowing my words. Deacon laughed uncomfortably, aware that he had already set our date out on the wrong path by choosing the worst place in the bar to sit.

When Deb finally placed two mugs of beer in front of us, Deacon drained his first beer and passed the empty mug to her. Instead of taking the empty vessel to the sink, Deb stood there, her hands braced against the bar, and smiled at us. Between the noise in the bar and my mother playing watchman over us, I knew our date was going to be doomed to failure. Not that I had high expectations for the situation.

"*Let's go sit in the restaurant!*" I shouted to Deacon. "*We can get some food to go with our drinks!*"

Glancing at my mother, Deacon gave me an appreciative nod before grabbing his mug. He gave Deb a smile and slid from his stool before walking away towards the restaurant. I turned to Deb and glowered at her.

"Get a life, Deb!"

She cackled as I hopped from my stool and followed after Deacon.

Fortunately, Deacon's seat choosing skills were better once we got to the other side of the building. He chose my favorite booth in the back corner and slid into the side facing the wall. Mirroring him, I slid into the seat across from him, my back to the wall. As I liked, this left me with a clear view of Harper's. I could see anyone coming or going.

After nearly getting stabbed by Prescott Pemberton's murderer, then getting shot at in the woods by Myrna Nelson to scare me off another case, I liked to have my back to walls. I'd never been a paranoid person, but the last few months had changed my views on certain things a bit. Enjoying a seat where no one could sneak up on me was a byproduct of those changing views.

"Jeez," Deacon groaned as he settled into his seat across from me, "Head Rock Harborians sure love John Denver."

"Is that what we call the people here?" I asked, setting my beer mug on the table. "I've wondered my whole life."

He shrugged. "I've been trying a few names."

"Head Rockers?" I suggested.

"Harbor Folk?" Deacon replied.

"Rockers?"

"HRHers?"

"Let's just call them 'Iowans' and be done with it," I said.

Deacon chuckled. "Agreed. But if you come up with something good, you'll have to let me know."

"I'll put it on my to-do list."

Deacon gave me a nod and reached for a menu.

"Sorry about my mother," I said. "She's…invasive."

Deacon waved me off as he perused the menu. "My mom's the same. Fortunately, she's an accountant, so it's unlikely she'll have a chance to bother us on this date."

"Onion rings," I said.

"Huh?"

"The onion rings are good with beer," I explained. "The rings here are great. Beau knows what he's doing with the rings."

Deacon laid the menu next to his beer and leaned in with a smile.

"Onion rings indicate that you want a snack," he said. "Especially when shared. A snack indicates that you want to make sure you're not stuck eating a meal, which takes longer. You want a snack, which takes less time to eat, meaning you think this date won't last long."

I couldn't help but blush. Thinking about the potential length of our date hadn't actually been on my mind, but not committing to anything had been.

"That's not why I suggested rings," I said.

"Have you eaten dinner yet?" he asked.

"No."

"Then we should have a full meal." Deacon picked up the menu again with a grin. "I promise that I won't try to keep you from leaving if you get bored."

"I'm not worried about that," I said.

"Then what's the hurry?"

"There's no hurry."

"When's the last time you were on a date?" Deacon leaned in to ask.

The fact that I had to think about the last time I'd gone on a date brought heat to my cheeks. Remembering which year I'd graduated college, then subtracting a year—since the last date I'd gone on had been during my junior year—took more time than Deacon was willing to allow.

"That long, huh?" he asked. "No wonder your date etiquette isn't great."

I scoffed.

"Date etiquette?" I said, ignoring the cheering coming from the bar as *Take Me Home, Country Roads* died away. "I'm not the one who sat next to the jukebox."

"You got me there." Deacon laughed. "But that was a mistake. Not poor etiquette."

"One could say that they are one and the same," I said. "Especially when trying to impress the person you asked out."

"I'm not trying to impress you."

"Clearly not." I gestured vaguely to the room around us.

Deacon laughed uproariously and I couldn't help but grin at his easy laughter. The realization that agreeing to a date with Deacon hadn't been a completely horrible decision struck me. Even if nothing else came of it, at least the *kid* could banter.

"They sell nightcrawlers and minnows out the back door," I said. "Did you know that?"

"I didn't," Deacon said, his laughter sputtering to an end. "I thought that was just a joke."

"Only until around ten in the morning," I said with a shrug. "Most people take off fishing before then anyway."

"Good to know."

"I never come here before lunch," I said. "I want to give them time to wash their hands."

Deacon sputtered with laughter again.

"That's not a nice way to talk about your mother's business."

"I don't think I'm going to do any damage," I said, flicking my head towards the bar.

He shook his head and an easy smile bloomed on his face. Deacon reached up and pushed his hair back so that it laid over the back of his skull. The shaved sides of his head were exposed, making him look as though he had a mohawk he hadn't bothered to gel and set. Which was actually accurate. He did have a mohawk. It was just laying down on his head. With his white-blond hair, nearly luminescent pale skin, button nose, and hazel eyes, I couldn't help but find him adorable.

"So," he said, "are we going to have an actual meal or what?"

I sighed, as though put out.

"Well," I wrapped my fingers around the handle of my mug, "who's paying?"

"Do they have a kids' menu?" A worried look crossed Deacon's face as his eyes shot down to his menu comically.

It was my turn to laugh. As the noise erupted from my throat, my eyes caught movement by the front door. Jeremy had entered Harper's, his eyes scanning the room innocently. When he heard my laugh, his head turned lazily towards the booth we were sitting in, and our eyes connected. I swallowed the laugh as Jeremy's eyes lit up and a small smile began to bloom on his face. When his eyes flicked over, catching the back of Deacon's head, the smile faltered. His face became a blank slate.

As I was contemplating smiling and waving at him—simply to keep the peace—Officer Ashley Riley walked in behind him, decked out in Saturday night clothes. He jovially slapped Jeremy on the back as he pushed his way in through the front door. Jeremy turned quickly towards the bar, but not so fast that I didn't catch the sullen frown that had immediately replaced his smile. I looked back to Deacon, hoping that he hadn't caught my sudden change in expression. When I locked eyes with my date, he was looking at me quizzically.

"It wasn't that funny?" he asked.

Doing some mental gymnastics, I veered my course back to my date.

"If you don't spend at least five dollars on my meal, I'll feel cheap," I said.

Deacon chuckled. "Okay, okay. I suppose I can let you order off the adult menu."

Smiling at each other, I did my best to forget the look I'd exchanged with Jeremy. Deacon and I exchanged a few more witty quips before Cleo showed up at our tableside to take our order. Following my lead—and expertise with the menu—Deacon chose to have the same thing I ordered. A cheesesteak with rings and coleslaw on the side. We both decided to switch to sodas to drink with our meal. Obviously, neither of us were interested in getting intoxicated.

Though I knew I could eat the meal I'd ordered in under twenty minutes if needed, I found myself taking my time. As

Deacon and I discussed work, our hobbies, made jokes, and then talked about books—my favorite topic of all time—I found that I didn't mind his company. There are worse things than a good meal and a good conversation with a cute guy on a Saturday night. If you find yourself in such a situation, it's best to enjoy it and not rush.

That was becoming my new motto, anyway.

By the time we were done eating—which included sharing a slice of pecan pie with vanilla ice cream—we'd spent two hours in Harper's. Though there was no reason to end the night early, when Cleo delivered the check, Deacon immediately paid. He left a forty-percent tip, which did impress me. Being polite to waitstaff and tipping them well is a surefire way to make me not dislike a person.

When Deacon slid from the booth after paying, I had begun to wonder if I'd done something to make him want to end the date early. Which annoyed me. I'd come to Harper's out of what I felt was an obligation to live up to our agreed upon arrangement. Feeling I'd been rejected annoyed me in ways I couldn't explain. However, when Deacon indicated we should go for a walk, I realized that he wasn't simply trying to get away from me.

Ego still intact!

Leaving Harper's, Deacon and I walked around Head Rock Harbor proper. A few times around the square, past The Dock and the police department, up to the actual harbor, past Munchies, and down Harbor Street. As we walked, I explained the plans and locations for all of the Pride Weekend events and what to expect. Deacon listened thoughtfully, interjecting his thoughts as we strolled along.

By the time we found ourselves in front of Head Rock Harbor Books, we were the only people on the street and the moon was shining full above us. The pools of yellow light from the street lamps on either end of the bookstore felt like spotlights for the end scene of a surprisingly successful first date.

"Well," I said with a sigh, stuffing my hands in my pockets, "this is me."

I jerked my head towards the shop.

"You live here?" Deacon asked. "I had no idea."

I rolled my eyes playfully.

"I had a good time," Deacon said, looking down as he kicked at the sidewalk adorably with the toe of his shoe. "I'm glad we did this."

"Me too," I replied. "Thanks for dinner. Best free cheesesteak ever."

We stood there for a moment, me staring at Deacon as he stared at his feet. Obviously, Deacon was good at dates, but not ending them. I couldn't actually say that I was in good practice with the ritual, either.

"Well," I said, "I'm definitely not a 'do you want to come up for a coffee' on the first date kind of guy, but…maybe a hug will do?"

Deacon chuckled, finally looking up at me.

"I really had a good time," he said. "I kind of don't want to say 'goodnight' is all."

The corner of my mouth quirked against my will.

"We'll have to do it again," I said.

"*Do it again* for real, or *do it again* as in *leave me alone so I can get inside*?" Deacon teased.

"I'll pay next time," I said.

"Okay." Deacon beamed at me.

I held my arms out, offering an end-of-the-night hug. Deacon stepped forward and accepted the embrace. Though I'd been close to him all night, I hadn't realized that Deacon actually smelled really good. Of course, not having a date in years, and having little physical contact with another man in as long, my olfactory senses might have been messing with me. I decided to simply enjoy the sensory overload. We stared at each other for a moment as we held each other, then I slowly slid my arms from around Deacon. A bashful yet pleased grin pulled at the corners of his mouth.

I cleared my throat.

"You going to be okay to get home?" I asked. "I can get my car if—"

"No," he said, waving me off, grinning. "I'm not far."

I knew where Deacon lived. When you reside in a small town like Head Rock Harbor, you basically know where everyone in town lives. He had a less than three-minute walk to his apartment. However, it would have been rude of me not to offer him a ride. Besides, I found that I wasn't quite ready to say "goodnight" either.

That could have been the years without a date thing playing with my brain.

"Okay," I said, stepping towards the door of the shop. "Text when you get home?"

"Will do," Deacon stood rigidly and gave me a salute.

We were both still chuckling as he took off down the street, a spring in his step. I watched him walk down Harbor Street until he was swallowed by the darkness. Taking a deep breath, I found myself grinning as I let myself into the bookstore and found an annoyed Abyssinian waiting on me.

Chapter Two

Coffee is one of my greatest loves; an affair spanning twelve years of my life. Even when there wasn't a man clamoring for my attention, there was coffee. So, when I accepted the mug of black gold that Angel slid across the wood bar, I was pleased. Bringing the mug to my lips, I took a tentative, yet appreciative, sip of the steaming liquid. Smooth, smoky, and with a hint of chocolate and hazelnut, the dark roast was exactly what I needed on a Sunday morning.

Head Rock Harbor Books is closed on Sundays and Mondays. However, Angel Gomez had arrived early Sunday morning to brew a few sample coffees for me to try. A kind of "test run" for the new coffee bar that would soon be open inside the shop. Angel, a recent arrival to the town of Head Rock Harbor, had applied for the position I'd posted in the front window of the shop at the beginning of May.

With no idea how to start, operate, or deal with a coffee bar, an experienced barista was a must. Angel had arrived in town at an opportune time. He had a knack for that, I was discovering. On a Sunday morning after a Saturday night date, having someone brew samples of coffee for you while you sat and relaxed was heaven.

"It's delicious," I said, lowering the mug to the bar.

Aside from running the bookstore and dealing with my personal life, for the last few weeks I'd been dealing with the back right corner of the store being in a perpetual state of disarray. I'd hired Sawyer to build a small coffee bar. A row of cabinets along the back corner, painted a gorgeous slate blue were topped with a dark walnut stained butcher's block. An espresso machine and various coffee making accoutrement sat atop it.

A four-foot-wide working area between the back wall of cabinets and the bar was lined with a rubber mat to make working on his feet easier for Angel. The front bar mirrored the back working space in color and composition, but the cabinets faced inward—extra storage for my new employee. A metal sign, cut out by Sawyer himself, was hung on the brick wall over the back counter. Fairy lights illuminated it from behind. It simply read "Head Rock Harbor Books Coffee Bar."

Not incredibly creative, but it got the job done.

"Those are my favorite beans for a simple cup of coffee," Angel explained, bracing his hands against the wooden bar. He smiled broadly, pleased that he'd chosen a coffee that I enjoyed. "For the frou-frou coffee drinks, I'll use something cheaper."

I chuckled and lifted the mug to my lips again.

Saving money on coffee beans wasn't going to immediately make up for the cost of installing a coffee bar in the bookstore, but it was a start. Between the permits, the cost of paying Sawyer to build the bar, and then having an actual employee on the payroll, my head was reeling. *I had an employee. I had to do more complicated payroll. What if no one wanted to get their coffee from us?* Walking into a bookstore to get coffee on Harbor Street was a lot less convenient than going through the drive-thru out on the highway.

Fast food coffee wasn't all that great—it was awful even. However, convenience often won out over quality when people are in a rush to get to work. Or wherever they're going when coffee is required. I swallowed my doubts and fears, along with the delicious second sip of coffee, and took time to examine the mug.

"Head Rock Harbor Books" was emblazoned in maroon on the white mug. A logo, which was basically a silhouette of Rattlesnatches atop a pile of books, sat in the middle of the name of the store.

"Do we really need branded mugs?" I thought out loud.

Angel nodded effusively.

"Once people realize they can sit and enjoy a cup of coffee with the book they just bought, we'll save a ton on disposable cups. And it's better for the environment," Angel explained excitedly. "And, once people *really* get invested in our awesome coffee, they'll want to buy a branded mug. We can sell them then."

I shrugged. "You're the expert."

I made a mental note to make a visit to The Loft and talk to Ainsley Bucksworth about a couple of easy chairs to tuck away in the coffee corner. If she wasn't as expensive as I imagined, I'd love to give a local business my money. Especially one on Harbor Street. However, a thrift shop in

Dubuque would get my money if Ainsley felt too proud of her wares.

Angel pushed back from the bar to stand proudly before me. In his skinny jeans with rips at the knees, his hip sneakers, white tank top, loose fitting light gray cardigan, black glasses, and wool beanie dangling precariously from the back of his head, he looked every bit the hipster barista. His copper skin made him look like he'd spent every waking moment of the beginning of summer on the river. He'd fit in well in Head Rock Harbor—even if his clothes were a little too hip.

"What's next?" I asked, sipping the coffee again.

I didn't want the coffee to cool too much before finishing the quarter-pour I'd been given from the French press.

"Hazelnut latte?" Angel asked.

"Bring it on!" I cheered goofily, slamming the last dregs of coffee in the mug.

An hour later, after trying seven different coffee drinks Angel prepared, I was practically vibrating on the sidewalk outside of Head Rock Harbor Books. Rattlesnatches was sitting in the window, practically shaking his head with disgust at me as I struggled to keep my hand steady enough to lock the door. Angel stood beside me, waiting for me to complete the Herculean task.

"So...when do we officially start?" Angel asked once I'd locked the door and turned to him.

I hoped my pupils weren't the size of dinner plates and my hair hadn't lost its curl to stand on end.

"Next week? After Pride is over," I said. "Let's have you in Tuesday through Saturday? Six to two? You can take a paid thirty-minute lunch in there sometime. We'll figure out which time is best as we go. I'll get word out that the coffee bar will officially be open this coming week."

By "get the word out" I meant that I'd tell Charlene Hardy. The president—*a job no one wanted*—of the Head Rock Harbor Business Association—*a barely existent organization*—was a notorious gossip.

Angel smiled and held out his hand.

"Sounds great," he said, beaming at me.

I took his hand.

"Thanks so much, Jackson," he continued. "It's not like there're tons of jobs here, you know? How lucky was it that I got here just as you wanted to open a coffee bar?"

"When it's meant to be…" I trailed off with a shrug as I shook his hand.

Angel and I took a few moments to discuss getting him a key to the bookstore. I wouldn't be venturing down from my apartment until nine each morning to deal with book sales. Angel needed a way to get into the store to start coffee sales at six. Having his own key to the main part of the bookstore was the only logical solution. We made a plan to talk on the phone later about how to deal with early morning coffee drinkers who might try to also buy books before I came downstairs for the day.

After exchanging a few pleasantries and saying our goodbyes, Angel and I went our separate ways. He headed west on Harbor Street, presumably back to his apartment in the newer complex on the far-west side of town. Even though it was late May, the weather was pleasant enough for a stroll through town. The breeze coming off the river was keeping the weather more than tolerable.

Once Angel was out of sight, I pulled my phone from my pocket and checked my messages. Deacon hadn't texted me the previous night when he got home, and having Angel see me thirstily checking my phone was out of the question. Obviously, it was okay that Deacon had forgotten to let me know he'd arrived home safely. He was a grown man—and people forget things sometimes. However, I couldn't help but feel a little slighted at the fact he'd forgotten so easily.

I pushed my feelings of rejection away and slid my phone into my pocket. If I wasn't going to text him out of fear of looking desperate, I certainly wasn't going to hold it against him for not texting me. Maybe he felt the same way—that a text so soon after the date would appear too much. It wasn't as if either of us had ended the date feeling we'd found the love of our lives or anything. But it hurt that he hadn't followed up with a text as promised.

Then again, you could text him, Jackson. I shook my head to clear my mind.

I headed east on Harbor Street, passing Charlene's Chocolates and The Loft, and entered Pain. Henry Mathis, the head baker and owner of Pain, was more than happy to sell me a loaf of his delicious jalapeno cheddar bread. I took a few moments to catch up with him before leaving and heading out east on Harbor Street once more. Hooking a right at the end of the block before getting to Munchies Café, I headed south towards the square.

A moment later, I was standing in front of The Downtown Theater. The English Storybook was one of the more unique buildings in all of Head Rock Harbor. The outside architecture was simply a façade, however. Inside was a ticket booth and lobby, like any traditional theater. Further into the building was a theater with a stage and a screen.

In years past, The Downtown Theater was a one-screen theater that showed one movie nightly and twice on Saturday and Sunday. Movies were switched out twice a month. Old timers around town still talked about the olden days when they frequented The Downtown Theater. Unfortunately, it had closed before I was old enough to have experienced it as a young citizen of Head Rock Harbor.

For over twenty years, The Downtown Theater had sat boarded up, vacant, and unused. For most of the citizens of Head Rock Harbor, it was nostalgic—but to others, it was an eyesore. A blemish on the quaint façade of downtown Head Rock Harbor. For me, it was a mixture of both. It was nostalgic in that I longed to have been able to visit The Downtown Theater, but its disuse and disrepair gave it a spooky, meth-lab feel to the rest of downtown. Luckily, everything was going to change.

The wooden sign that hung next to the front walkway was gone, and a white banner with red lettering now hung proudly over the front door.

Harbor Stage – Opening Soon!
New Management!

To everyone's shock and delight, a married couple from "back east" had purchased The Downtown Theater at the beginning of May. Their intention, from what the gossip around town declared, was to reopen The Downtown Theater—with a new name, of course—and a new mission. They wanted to bring live theater to Head Rock Harbor. Of course, only people from "back east" would be brave enough for such a venture in a small town.

Personally, I applauded them.

The couple, Michael and Randall Cummings, had been spending the last month renovating the theater and getting it up to code. The outside, having been in pretty decent shape, began to look as glorious as it had in its heyday fairly quickly. I'd yet to see the inside of the theater, and it had become a mission of mine to be one of the first—if not the first—Head Rock Harbor citizen to get a sneak peek.

Strolling up to the front door of Harbor Stage—whose name everyone in town would surely struggle with for months—I knocked on the front door. Being a business, I couldn't decide if knocking first or walking right in was appropriate. Since the Cummings hadn't opened for business yet, I decided that knocking first was best. With the loaf of jalapeno cheddar bread cradled in my arm, I stepped back and waited patiently.

Nearly a minute passed with no answer, and I was reaching for the door handle, before it finally swung inward. Shocked by the sudden opening of the door, I took another step back, nearly falling off of the front porch of the building. Correcting my stance and chuckling nervously, I looked up to find a middle-aged man standing in the doorway of Harbor Stage. He was looking at me quizzically, a ghost of a smile on his face.

I couldn't blame him. Anyone nearly falling is a little humorous—as long as they aren't hurt.

"Can I help you?" The man asked evenly, making an obvious effort to remove the amused smile from his face.

"You scared me," I said, chuckling. "I don't make it a habit to stumble everywhere I go."

"Well, I'm sure your insurance company will be happy to hear that," he replied.

He held out his hand.

"Michael Cummings," he said as I took the offered hand and shook it.

"Jackson Harper," I replied. "I own the—"

"Head Rock Harbor Books," Michael said, nodding happily. "Charlene Hardy told us about you and your store."

"Hopefully, it was all good."

My response was meant as a joke, but finding out the things Charlene said behind my back would have been interesting. Michael let go of my hand and leaned against the jamb of the door.

"I've been meaning to come into your bookstore," he said. "I've heard wonderful things. With the renovations, though—"

He gestured vaguely at the building behind him.

"Oh," I said, "no worries. I know what it's like starting a new business. Even if renovations aren't necessary. I just did some remodeling in the shop."

"Oh?"

"Put in a coffee bar," I said. "People have been suggesting it for a while, and there's no real coffee shop downtown proper, so…"

"I'm sure it will be a boon to the community," Michael said, his "back east" accent apparent.

I didn't know which state "back east" he was from, but his accent was decidedly not Midwestern. If I'd had to guess, I would have placed him as a native New Yorker. Besides, that's usually what folks in Head Rock Harbor mean when they say "back east"—someone is from New York.

"I know you haven't had a lot of time to check out all the shops," I began, removing the loaf of bread from the crook of my arm," and I wanted to welcome you to town. This is from Pain. The bakery on Harbor Street. Henry Mathis is a wonderful baker."

Michael accepted the loaf from me graciously, his eyes lighting up at the sight of the bread.

"We're all really excited to have The Downtown Theater—um, Harbor Stage—back in use. So, anything I can do to make you feel welcome and not leave."

He laughed and examined the loaf a moment longer before tucking it into the crook of his arm, mirroring my method of carrying it.

"That's very kind of you, Jackson," he said. "Thank you."

"You're welcome," I said. "Is Randall here? I haven't met him yet."

Michael's face bloomed into a smile.

"And yet you know his name," Michael said, shaking his head.

"Small towns." I shrugged and chuckled.

Michael's smile didn't disappear, but he seemed to be sizing me up, as if unsure about something. Finally, he seemed to make a decision and spoke.

"I noticed the rainbow sticker in your front window when I walked by the other day," he said cryptically.

"Yeah," I said. "I'm a queer business owner, too."

His smile finally seemed genuine.

"It's a small town," I said, trying to assuage his obvious fears. "But we're all pretty much live and let live around here. As long as you can take what some of the older folks consider humor."

Michael laughed then.

"Been doing that my whole life," he said, standing up straight. "And I just wanted to know if I should refer to Randall as my partner or husband."

"Too late for that. The prayer chain has already got your business all over town."

Laughing harder, Michael shook his head.

"This will be an adjustment," he said.

"So," I asked again, "is Randall here?"

Michael shook his head, a look of concern crossing his face.

"He left early this morning for a run," Michael replied. "He said he was going to run and check out the town some more, and—"

Michael's abrupt end to his speech and the fact that he was looking over my shoulder had me turning to see what his eyes had landed on. Jogging up the walkway to the Harbor Stage porch was a tall, lanky man clad in black basketball shorts, a white tank top, and black sneakers. As he approached, I noticed the earbuds in his ears.

A shock of red hair that flopped to one side of his head and a lightly freckled face displayed a confused, but delighted smile. Around forty-five years old—like Michael, if my age-guessing skills were accurate—Randall was an attractive man. As was Michael. However, Randall, by my estimation, was what more people would consider "conventionally" attractive. Michael, on the other hand, in his khaki slacks, button-up short-sleeve shirt, and business casual shoes, dark brown hair with specks of gray, and dark eyes, was more for the sophisticated tastes.

As Randall approached, he reached up and plucked the earbuds from his ear. He pulled a phone from his pocket, pushing a few buttons—obviously to stop his music—and deposited the phone and earbuds back into his pocket. Breathing as though he had barely done any exercise at all, Randall approached us, stopping at the first step to Harbor Stage. I greeted him with a smile.

"Here he is now," Michael said from behind me. "He always likes to make an entrance."

Randall looked over at Michael and chuckled, then his eyes were back on me.

"We have company?" he asked his husband.

"This is Jackson," Michael replied. "The owner of Head Rock Harbor Books?"

Randall's eyes lit up and he dashed up the steps to stand with us on the porch. He held his hand out.

"Randall Cummings," he said. "Nice to meet you."

"Jackson Harper," I said, though it was redundant. "Nice to meet you, too."

"To what do we owe the pleasure?" Randall asked, raising a hand to wipe nonexistent sweat from his brow.

Although the action was obviously performative—it wasn't hot enough yet so early in the day, and Randall was obviously in great shape—I ignored it. He moved to stand next to Michael, so I turned back around to talk to them. Before I could speak, Michael answered for me.

"Jackson was kind enough to bring us a loaf of jalapeno cheddar bread from Pain," Michael said, bouncing the loaf still cradled in his arm. "And to welcome us. One queer business owner to others."

Michael and Randall exchanged glances and smiles, and the statement wasn't lost on me.

"Just wanted you to feel welcome," I said.

"That's very thoughtful of you, Jackson. Thank you." Randall smiled.

"Well, I did have an ulterior motive," I admitted.

"Oh?" Michael's brow rose on the left side.

Randall and him looked at each other quizzically.

"I was hoping to get a sneak peek at Harbor Stage," I said, unabashedly. "Be the first in town to see the new business opening."

Both men laughed jovially and Randall reached out to pat my shoulder.

"Well," he said, "for your honesty, I'm sure we can give you a quick tour."

"Don't expect much, though," Michael said, starting to turn towards the door. "We still have a lot to do before opening next month."

"We'd hoped to have everything ready for Pride, but things never work out the way you intend when it comes to starting a business," Randall added.

"You're preaching to the choir," I said with a laugh as we all headed to the door.

As Michael started inside, the squealing of tires and the sounds of "whoops" out on the street stopped us. In unison, the three of us spun around to see what all of the commotion was about. A parade of two convertibles and one pickup was racing down the road towards the harbor. The truck was pulling a boat big enough for fifteen people. All full of passengers, obviously having a great time and ignoring the fact that their loudness might not be welcome in our sleepy town, the vehicles raced by without a care.

Michael, Randall, and I all exchanged confused glances. When I spotted the rainbow flag fluttering from a pole on the back of the boat, I relaxed.

"Oh, no," Randall whispered comically from behind me. "The queers are in town for Pride."

I chuckled.

"Two queer business owners and an inaugural Pride parade and they come out in droves," Michael tutted.

The three of us shook our heads, laughing together. We all watched as the vehicles disappeared down the street in the direction of the harbor. Obviously, I'd expected out-of-town queer people to come to Head Rock Harbor for Pride. Especially those from smaller communities nearby where Pride events were scarce. I just hadn't expected them to arrive five days in advance.

"Well, I'm sure Lila Westbrook isn't upset," I said, then realized Randall and Michael had no idea what I was talking about. "She owns the Head Rock Harbor Inn?"

They both nodded, obviously catching my drift.

"Well, at least someone will benefit from the extra population for a week," Michael shrugged. "Come on, Jackson. Let's get that tour underway!"

Together, the three of us entered Harbor Stage. I practically wanted to rub my hands together devilishly at having pulled off my plan. Being the first person in Head Rock Harbor to get a gander at the new theater was going to make a lot of people jealous. And all it took was a delicious loaf of bread, some manners, and honesty.

Being a fellow queer business owner hadn't hurt, either.

Chapter Three

Monday morning in the bookstore was spent pulling my hair in frustration as I stared at my laptop screen at the checkout counter. The notes sent by my editor for the climax of *An Artful Assault*, the upcoming sixth book in the *Detective Randy Melton Mystery series*, made no sense. At least, not from a writer's or reader's standpoint. The changes she'd suggested would completely contradict evidence in earlier chapters. I had to wonder how closely she had actually paid attention to the book up until she got to the climax.

So close to finishing my edits and shipping them off to my editor and publisher, I was frustrated at the setback. Since sitting at the counter and tapping away mindlessly was going to get me nowhere fast, I opened my e-mail. After several bad attempts at professionalism, I finally composed a decent e-mail asking for clarification from my editor. I cc'd by publisher so as to keep them in the loop, and sent it on its way.

Before I could decide to use my laptop to bash my own head in, I saved the file, lowered the screen, and stored the device under the counter. Rattlesnatches, who'd been begging for extra attention for a month, saw his opportunity, suddenly leaping onto the check-out counter out of nowhere. Laughing at his display as he rolled on the counter playfully in front of me, I spent a few minutes giving him belly rubs and ear scratches.

After a thorough kitty massage, I located the cat fishing pole I kept hidden under the counter. For the next half hour, the two of us played, him leaping at the feather and bell at the end of the fishing line as I laughed and played keep away, flicking the pole each time he got close. A half hour passed before Rattlesnatches decided he'd had enough of my shenanigans. Finally, he sauntered away, pleased with our quality time, and climbed to the top of the science fiction shelf to lay on one of his favorite perches.

Knowing I'd been dismissed, I hid the fishing pole under the counter once again and left the check-out counter. I climbed the stairs to the balcony outside of my studio apartment and plopped down in the chair by the entry. With nothing better to do on a lazy Monday, I pulled my current cross-stitch work in progress out of the basket beside the chair. I'd been working on a J.R.R. Tolkien inspired piece forever, and the last month had eaten into my hobby time. Getting an hour or two of uninterrupted work would move the piece along nicely.

No sooner had I done a row of stitches than I was interrupted. The sound of approaching sirens made me look up from my cross-stitch and stare out the windows of the shop below. Distant at first, the sirens grew closer, getting progressively louder as I frowned and stared down at Harbor Street through the windows. When it didn't seem the sirens could get any louder, flashing lights filled the front of the shop and an ambulance whizzed by. I leapt from my seat as the ambulance disappeared and the sirens started to fade again, the lights disappearing from the shop.

When more sirens suddenly sounded and more lights filled the shop, my brow furrowed as a fire truck whipped by the shop. Thoroughly concerned, my worry only grew when the fire truck disappeared, only to be replaced by the sight of Jeremy's car flying by the front of the shop. A flash of black following all the red and white.

Depositing my cross-stitch in the basket by the chair, I hurried down the stairs and rushed to grab my keys and wallet from the check-out counter. Not considering that I was getting involved in something that was none of my business, I faced out the back of the shop. Popping out into the alley from the backdoor, I leapt into my red Beetle and took off. By the time I'd pulled out of the alley and rounded the building onto Harbor Street, I could barely hear the sirens.

Fortunately, I'd been quick enough getting in the Beetle that all of the emergency vehicles hadn't gotten so far that I couldn't spot their lights. They'd turned at the corner and gone south towards Wilford Woods. Immediately, my stomach knotted up and my heart sank as I remembered finding Carter Nelson's body. If there was another hurt—*or dead*—person in the woods, I wasn't certain I wanted to know.

I sat there in the Beetle, my hands gripping the steering wheel tightly for a moment, trying to decide if I shouldn't repark the car and go back in the shop. Curiosity got the better of me, and I found my foot hitting the gas. Speeding away from Head Rock Harbor Books, I sped to the corner, hooked a right—completely ignoring the stop sign—and chased after the lights.

The trip south wasn't long. I'd traveled a mere two blocks before I found the emergency vehicles congregating in the parking lot of The Dock. Jeremy was hopping out of his car when I pulled into the lot. Distracted by whatever had brought him and the other emergency personnel to The Dock, Jeremy didn't even notice the Beetle peeling in behind them. By the time I'd parked and hopped out of my car, Jeremy had made his way from his car and around the side of the restaurant.

A quick glance around and I saw that the EMS and firefighters were pulling a gurney from the back of the ambulance. The speed—or lack thereof—with which they were unloading the gurney let me know that they were not present to save a life. My gut twisted up in panic, and I nearly slid back into the Beetle. Somehow, my curiosity won out over my anxiety, and I found myself hustling across the parking lot towards the side of The Dock where Jeremy had disappeared.

The firefighters and EMS glanced up when I dashed by, but most of them smiled and waved. Another thing about growing up and living in a small town—everyone knows you, so you never look out of place. In a big city, one of the emergency personnel might have stopped me. Questioned what business I had being at an obvious crime scene. The guys with the ambulance and firetruck assumed I had a valid reason to be present.

Rounding the side of the restaurant, I caught sight of Jeremy at the base of the hill that sloped down the side of

The Dock and to the sandbar behind it. The partly grassy and partly rocky hill bled into the sandy jut of land that stretched out twenty feet into the river. Jeremy was making his way across the sand, shaking his feet with each step. Obviously, sand and dress shoes do not mix. Before I headed down the hill, I looked out across the sandbar to see what I might be getting myself into by following.

Out where the river met the sand, Marv and Officer Riley were standing near a large beach umbrella, staked into the sandbar. The umbrella was angled so that I could only see the striped top, and the upper half of Marv's and Officer Riley's bodies. I couldn't tell what lay under the umbrella, but logic told me what would be found.

As I started down the hill, I alternated between glancing down to make sure I didn't stumble over rocks, and glancing up to keep an eye on the activity out at the sandbar. By the time I got to the base of the hill and my sneakers touched sand, Jeremy was already out at the tip of the sandbar, standing behind the umbrella with Marv and Riley. He crouched out of viewed as I began making my way across the sandbar.

Before I could get to the umbrella, Marv happened to look up and his eyes landed on me. To say that his expression was unimpressed was putting things mildly. Annoyed would have been a better descriptor for his expression, but it still wouldn't have quite nailed it. He said something to the men with him that the wind whipping along the river kept me from hearing, and Jeremy popped up from behind the umbrella. He didn't give me the same look as Marv, but he didn't seem pleased to see me, either.

"Jackson!" Marv barked as I approached. "What on God's green ball of crap are you doing here?"

"Saw the lights and heard the sirens," I said. "Decided to come join the party?"

He glared at me. Officer Riley seemed unbothered. Jeremy frowned.

"And what made you think your presence was needed?" he asked.

I shrugged, having no answer for that question.

"I don't remember deputizing you," Marv grumbled. "And if someone sent you an *honorary detective badge*, I don't remember authorizing it."

He didn't mean to, I could tell, but he shot eyes at Jeremy. Fortunately, Jeremy was too busy frowning at me to catch the jab.

"I'm not useless in murder investigations," I stated the obvious. "In case you've somehow forgotten."

Marv rolled his eyes and crossed his arms over his chest.

"How do you know there's been any crime?" he asked. "Let alone a *murder*?"

"Well, the guys up there," I said, gesturing to the parking lot behind me, "are taking their sweet time getting the gurney ready. Tell's me that they're not here trying to *save* a life."

The corner of Jeremy's mouth quirked up, but the expression quickly disappeared.

"Aren't you just—" Marv began.

"You need to leave, Jackson," Jeremy interjected. "You don't need to see this. Go back up that hill, and go back to the store."

Taking my turn to frown, I couldn't help but wonder why Jeremy was taking Marv's side so easily. Typically, my best friend did his best to stay on his boss's good side, which I understood, but he was never so pointed with it. Especially going so far as to interrupt Marv. Telling me to "go back to the store" with such vehemence made me even more curious as to what was behind the umbrella. Actually, I knew what was behind the umbrella, I simply became more curious as to how bad it could be.

"What is it?" I asked only loudly enough to be heard over the wind.

Marv's and Jeremy's expressions changed from annoyed to concerned and they exchanged a glance. Riley was still looking down at whatever lay behind the umbrella. Before Marv and Jeremy could come to a decision on how to deal with me, I rushed over and rounded the umbrella. Both of them groaned with dismay as I pushed between them to look under the umbrella.

I nearly stumbled back at the sight of the body that lay before us. Marv and Jeremy reached out in tandem to grab ahold of me so that I wouldn't stumble back into the water rear first. However, it wasn't the stab wounds and the alarming amount of blood that covered the body that shocked me. The man's white-blond hair swooped to the side of his head was like a punch to the gut. Even with Jeremy and Marv holding me up, it was nearly impossible to keep myself upright.

Chapter Four

Since I'd already seen the body, Marv and Jeremy hadn't bothered making me leave the crime scene. However, I was shoved out of the way to the other side of the sandbar so that they could work and the emergency crew wouldn't have me in the way as they collected the body. I was sitting in the sand, my knees pulled up to my chest with my arms wrapped around them. My chin was resting on my knee and I was looking anywhere besides at the umbrella.

Even though my current position was such that the umbrella was blocking my view of the body, simply looking in its direction made the image of the body flash through my mind. Flashes of red flooded my mind as I thought of that swoop of hair. Bile threatened to rise up in my throat as I squeezed my eyes shut. If I could close them tightly enough, maybe I could unsee the carnage under that umbrella.

When trying to chase the images from my head failed, I opened my eyes and turned my head to stare out at the water. The river, never unmoving, though not always roaring, was flowing peacefully by—or as peacefully as the Mississippi can get. Moving into summer, the cool breeze flowing along the river was surprising. Early June in Iowa is rarely sweltering, but having such a cool day was a rarity.

I stared at the water, wondering what the summer had in store for us. With Pride coming, there'd be plenty of activities to keep my mind busy in the coming weeks. Head Rock Harbor had plenty of weekend events throughout the season to keep tourists pouring into town and the shops busy. Before I knew it, summer would be gone and I'd be planning my autumn activities and breaking out my winter gear once again.

Trying to think of anything besides the carnage a few yards away was the only way I knew how to deal with what I'd seen. Even though I'd seen more crime scenes and dead bodies than was typical for an average person, I now knew that I'd never get used to it. A life ended through violence was something that a normal person should always find disturbing.

At least I could say I was *normal*. Always look for the silver lining.

"You okay?"

I jerked, startled by the sound, and whipped my head around to find Jeremy crouching down in front of me. As soon as our eyes connected, a shiver ran up my spine, and I couldn't stop it. My whole body shuddered. Jeremy smiled empathetically and cautiously reached out, laying a hand on my shoulder.

"Are you okay, Jacks?" he asked again.

Swallowing down the bile that still threatened to gush up my throat, I managed to nod.

"You sure?" Jeremy squeezed my shoulder.

"Yeah," I croaked. "Yes."

My eyes darted over to the umbrella right as Deacon popped up, a red hazardous waste baggie in his hand. Fixated on his task, he worked meticulously to seal the baggie as he stared at its contents. The white-blond swoop of hair laying to the side of his head made my throat clench harder. Jeremy followed my eyes and his hand slid from my shoulder.

"I thought the same thing," he said, his voice emotionless. "When I first got here. Even though I knew it wasn't him and he was on his way to the scene. The resemblance..."

I didn't respond, but my eyes moved to stare at the sand at my feet.

"But there's Deacon," Jeremy said. "He's fine."

If I'd only waited to inject myself into the crime scene—even three minutes—I wouldn't have been as started by what I'd found under the umbrella. I'd barely seen the victim and registered what I was looking at before Deacon arrived on the scene. Those two or three minutes between seeing the crime scene and Deacon arriving had been enough to shake me to my core.

"I thought...you know," I said.

Eloquence was obviously abandoning me for the time being.

"I know," Jeremy said.

He tried to sound compassionate, but his voice sounded hollow.

"Obviously," I squeaked out, "it wasn't."

"It wasn't," Jeremy said, reinforcing the fact for me.

"But who is it, then?" I asked. "I didn't...recognize him."

Jeremy shook his head slowly side to side.

"Germ..."

"This isn't me playing the contentious cop and keeping you from details about the case," Jeremy said. "I honestly have no idea. Never seen him before. But the way he's messed up…no. I still don't know. I only know one person with that haircut and it's obviously not him. Must not be a local."

I nodded. "Okay."

I pulled my knees to my chest and wrapped my arms around them again. Jeremy laid a tentative hand on my right forearm and gave it a squeeze.

"You probably need to leave," he said. "Not just because this is a crime scene—but because you're not handling this well. And you shouldn't be. No one should see what you've just seen."

"Okay," I said, surprising even myself at my agreeability.

"Okay?" Jeremy chuckled and squeezed my forearm again. "Just like that?"

I managed an amused sound and looked up at Jeremy.

Compassion filled Jeremy's expression again and he gave my forearm one last squeeze before pulling his hand away. Any other cop would have read me the Riot Act for how I'd behaved. Reminded me that I was putting my nose in business that was most certainly not mine. Not Jeremy. He wasn't going to rub salt in the wound.

"Lessons learned all around," Jeremy said.

He didn't have to explain what he meant.

"Yeah."

Without a word, Jeremy rose and held his hand out to me. I accepted the offering and rose to my feet. More sand slid into my shoes and I cringed. Jeremy looked down and chuckled. Turning me away from the water towards The

Dock, he patted me on the back, leading me away from the crime scene. When we got to the base of the craggy hill that led back up to the front of the restaurant, he stopped and faced me.

"Go home and shake your shoes out. Take a shower," Jeremy suggested. "Have something to eat and watch something silly on T.V. You'll feel better before you know it."

"Okay."

"I'll stop by later if you want?"

Having Jeremy in my apartment wasn't something I was sure I wanted since I felt so vulnerable, but I wasn't sure I wanted to be alone, either.

"Okay," I said.

He smiled broadly.

"See you soon, Jacks," Jeremy said, patting my back again. "Now go home and keep your nose out of police business. This time it's being said for your mental health. Okay?"

Nodding, I did my best to give him a smile. Jeremy turned and stomped through the sand back towards the umbrella and the crime scene team. As he rounded the umbrella, my eyes drifted to Deacon. He was looking at me. Our eyes connected and he pointed at himself discreetly, then made a phone out of his hand and held it to the side of his head before pointing at me.

I'll call you.

I nodded.

You better, I thought.

Not only did Deacon need to call me so that my mind would be at ease about what had transpired in the last half hour, but he owed me. He still hadn't even texted me since he'd gotten home Saturday night. Once I'd showered, ate, watched some T.V., and didn't feel like puking anymore, I had words for him. I'd get a reason for his rudeness one way or another. However, after the scare I'd had, I found I couldn't bring myself to be incredibly angry at him any longer.

As I made my way up the hill, avoiding the big rocks, the EMTs and firefighters were bringing the gurney down. I gave them a wide berth so as to not interfere any further in the crime scene, not stopping until I got to the top of the hill. Once I'd crested the top, I turned and gave the scene below another glance.

Jeremy, Marv, Deacon, and Ashley were all still standing around the crime scene, most of the victim blocked by the umbrella. I could see the man's body from mid-thigh down from my new vantage point—one I hadn't taken advantage of when I'd arrived at the scene. Now, I found myself staring at the man's bare feet and legs, and the bright orange of his swimming trunks. When Jeremy caught me staring from the top of the hill, he motioned for me to keep moving.

For once, I didn't ignore him to prove he wasn't the boss of me.

Back at the bookstore minutes later, I parked the Beetle and made my way inside. Rattlesnatches mewled at me when I passed by him on my way up the stairs, but he seemed to understand I needed a minute to myself. I made my way upstairs and began stripping off my clothes as soon as I was inside of my small apartment. Seconds later, I was standing under the hot stream of water in my shower, my hands braced against the tiled wall.

Though I was a person who was cognizant of environmental issues and didn't waste water, I took a much longer shower than was typical. By the time I stepped out of the shower, water dripping from the curls plastered to my skull, the hot water heater had lost its battle. Shivering, though not from cold, I dried off and slipped into a fresh pair of underwear, sweatpants, and a pocket t-shirt that was one size too large. I slid into my house slippers and began searching the fridge for something easy to make for an early lunch.

For once, I had no leftovers in the fridge to pop in my tiny microwave and reheat. Fortunately, I found a large plastic container of homemade potato and corn chowder pushed to the back of the freezer. I dumped the frozen block of chowder into a saucepan and let it start melting and heating slowly as I mixed up some cornbread batter. Once my cast iron skillet full of batter was in the oven, I chopped up some green onions that had been neglected in the fridge and were a day away from going bad.

Once the chowder was once again in a liquid-like form and steaming in the pot and the cornbread was done, I ladled a huge portion of the chowder into a bowl. I sprinkled the top with shredded cheddar and green onions. Then I plunked a large slice of the cornbread atop it all. Before anything else, I turned the T.V. stand to face my bed. Then I crawled into bed with the bowl, sitting up against the headboard.

By the time I was mixing the cornbread into the chowder, Rattlesnatches had made his way into the apartment. He leapt up onto the bed silently and laid across my feet over the covers. I flipped the T.V. on using the remote that lived on my bedside table and ate quietly as some stupid animated show played. The T.V. was more for noise to keep my mind from getting too loud. I didn't really pay much attention to it, and if asked later, wouldn't be able to tell anyone a single thing that happened in the show.

Before I knew it, my bowl was empty, my belly was full, and the T.V. show was ending. I turned the T.V. off and made a tongue clicking sound as I set the bowl on the bed beside me. Taking his cue, Rattlesnatches leapt from his spot across my feet and sauntered up to my offering. As his ruddy triangle-shaped head dipped into the bowl and he began lapping at the remains of my chowder, I stroked his back.

"Remember," I said, "we don't tell people we do this. We would be judged."

Rattlesnatches didn't lift his head from the bowl, but he began to purr.

"I don't know. Not everyone would think this is odd."

I nearly fell out of the bed at the sound of the voice from my apartment doorway. Jerking my head around, I found Jeremy walking into view, smiling at me. Holding my hand to my chest, a nervous laugh escaped my throat. Rattlesnatches hadn't even stopped licking at the bowl. No amount of shock on my part would have stopped him from chowing down.

"How'd you get in here?" I asked.

"I have a key." Jeremy laughed softly as he sauntered into the bedroom area, closer to my bed. "Why do you always forget things when you're startled?"

I shrugged.

Jeremy shook his head mirthfully and sat down at the end of the bed. Reaching out, he laid a hand atop my shin over the blanket.

"You feeling better?" he asked.

"I'm clean. I'm not hungry anymore," I said.

"You know what I mean," Jeremy said, squeezing my shin.

I sighed. "Yeah. That...that was gruesome."

Jeremy tilted his head and gave me a sympathetic look as his mouth scrunched up with worry. He looked as though he'd been disturbed by the scene as well. His golden curls looked as though he had been running his hands through them anxiously. Of course, even the most seasoned detective would never become accustomed to the atrocities humans commit against each other. At least, the most seasoned detectives who weren't psychotic.

"I've seen dead bodies, of course. But that was bad, Germ."

"It's definitely the worst I've seen. In person. I saw worse in college and the academy, but nothing like that here," Jeremy said. "I get it."

"Who could be that angry to...kill someone in such a way?" I asked, shaking my head. "Who could make someone angry enough to cause them to become that violent?"

Jeremy took his turn shaking his head as his hand slid from my shin. His fingers whispered along the fabric of my comforter. Rattlesnatches continued lapping at the bowl, though I was fairly certain it had to be spotless by now.

"Murder doesn't make sense, Jacks," Jeremy said. "You can figure out motive and all that, but in the end, people who are capable of that kind of thing aren't right in the head. There's no point in trying to logic it out."

"I suppose. But you'd have to have a pretty good motive to do *that* to someone."

"That's just you not wanting to believe some people simply suck," Jeremy said.

We sat in silence, both of us lost in our own thoughts as Rattlesnatches climbed into my lap and curled up into the cutest ruddy red ball anyone had ever seen.

"Look, Jacks," Jeremy began suddenly, "I came over here because I wanted to make sure you were okay after seeing that."

"I appreciate it."

"And I wanted to say—"

Before Jeremy could finish his thought, my phone began ringing and vibrating on my bedside table. He cut off in the middle of his statement as his eyes darted over to my phone making a nuisance of itself on the table. With an apologetic grimace, I held a finger up to my friend and snatched my phone off of the table. Unbothered by the sound, Rattlesnatches continued to purr in my lap, his belly full of chowder leavings.

"It's Deacon," I said, glancing at my phone screen.

Jeremy's face went blank as he stared at me holding the still ringing phone.

"Well," he said, standing from the bed, "don't leave him waiting. I have to get going anyway."

"Germ, I—"

"I'm glad you're okay, Jacks," he said, making his way to the apartment door. "Call me later or something. Okay?"

He gave me a small wave and then exited the apartment into the bookstore. Frowning to myself, I tapped the screen of my phone to accept the call. I could hear Jeremy's footsteps on the stairs as I brought the phone to my ear.

"Hello?" I asked.

I always felt funny saying "hello" when answering the phone if it was someone in my contacts calling. Obviously, I knew who was calling. Why not answer with a more personalized greeting? Social norms still forced us all to sound inquisitive when answering our phones in one of the greatest technology eras in human history. One day I was going to lean into the phenomenon of social norms not keeping up with technology and answer all of my calls with a spritely "Ahoy-hoy!" I'd try to wait until I was old enough to be considered eccentric instead of crazy.

"*Hey, Jackson.*" Deacon's voice came through the phone.

It wasn't fair. As the person on the other end of the phone being answered, he got to acknowledge he knew who he was speaking with at present.

"Hey, Deacon," I replied.

"*Are you okay?*"

"Too many people are asking me that lately." I couldn't help but chuckle. "Yeah. I'm fine."

Deacon laughed with me for a moment.

"*It was pretty messed up,*" Deacon admitted. "*Even I wanted to sling some hash.*"

Knowing what I knew of Deacon's proclivity for creative euphemisms and slang, I assumed he meant that he had felt nauseated at the crime scene.

"Yeah," I replied. "I just had lunch, but I'm holding it down okay. We'll see what happens."

"*Hey,*" Deacon said, "*I wanted to apologize for not texting the other night.*"

"And yesterday?" I reminded him.

He chuckled nervously. "*And yesterday. I nearly fell down the stairs going up to my apartment Saturday night and*"

I dropped my phone and shattered it. Then I took Mom to church on Sunday and then I had to drive into Dubuque to get a new phone and by the time I got home—"

"It's fine," I said, stopping him. "Really. I get it."

There was no point in reminding Deacon he could have stopped by the store. Or used someone else's phone. Or a landline—if those still existed. A note taped to the bookstore door would have worked as well. Was I the only twenty-seven-year-old alive who understood that things could be done without the newest technology?

"Well, I offer my sincerest apologies and hope that I will stay within your good graces. I know you have it in you to forgive me. Someone so handsome is surely as attractive inside."

I decided I could forgive Deacon, but I couldn't let him know immediately.

"My aunt Belinda would have said you're so full of it your eyes are brown, Deacon," I responded playfully.

"But my eyes are hazel. That's impossible."

"Fine, fine," I replied. "You're forgiven, I suppose."

"Okay," Deacon said. *"Because I really did have a good time the other night. I don't want to ruin my chances of a second date."*

"That all depends," I teased. "Do I still have to pay next time?"

"It's negotiable," Deacon chuckled.

We spent a few more minutes on the phone, teasing each other, before we finally ended the call with a promise to text and plan a second date. By the time I hung up the phone, my mood had improved considerably. Knowing that Deacon was okay—especially knowing that he wasn't the victim under the umbrella—had saved the day. The knowledge that he hadn't simply been avoiding texting or calling me because he had actually hated our date had a smile plastered to my face.

I was setting my phone back on the bedside table when Rattlesnatches' ears perked up, though he didn't move from my lap. Tilting my head to the side, I realized I'd also heard something. It took a moment for me to realize the distant tinkling sound had been the bell over the door in the shop below. Cautiously, I slid out of the bed, nudging Rattlesnatches to the side.

On tiptoes, I crept to the apartment door and made my way out onto the balcony that overlooked the shop. The lights were still out and I quickly scanned the shop, finding no one lurking. When I looked over at the door, the bell over it was still swaying gently. When my eyes darted to the window, I saw a flash of golden curls before Jeremy completely disappeared from sight.

My eyes narrowed as I stared at the window, though there was no longer anything to see. Had he been in the shop the whole time I'd been on the phone with Deacon? *Had he stayed behind to eavesdrop on my private phone call?* Scowling deeply, I marched back into my apartment and snatched my phone from the bedside table. I'd opened the messaging app to shoot off an accusatory message to my best friend, but stopped myself.

Deacon had mentioned he had a lot of work to do now that he was in the lab. Surely, Jeremy had tons of work to begin his investigation. Even angry and confused at what I'd seen through the window, I didn't want to put him in a sour mood for the rest of his work day. There would be plenty of time to tear into him about his nosiness later.

So, I shot off a different kind of text.

Munchies during lunch break tomorrow? My treat.

I knew Jeremy well enough to know that if there was an offer of free food, he'd show up. Then I'd have him in a booth across from me to chastise for what he'd done. I set my phone back on the bedside table, knowing he wouldn't respond immediately, and went down to retrieve my laptop from under the check-out counter. By the time I was sliding back into bed, I realized I couldn't really do any writing until I heard from my editor, so I laid it next to me on the bed.

As I was turning on the T.V. to watch something else while tucked comfortably in bed, my phone chimed. A glance over at the screen let me know that Jeremy had responded. I didn't bother picking up my phone and opening the messages. The message he'd sent was short enough to show up on the banner popup.

See you then, his text read.

Oh, I thought, *you'll see me then, mister.*

Chapter Five

With the forecast calling for warmer weather in the coming days, I wasn't entirely shocked when the rain began to patter down Monday evening. Bedtime was approaching and Rattlesnatches had already taken up his place in the middle of my bed and began his nightly grooming routine. I'd gone into the bathroom off of the kitchen in my little efficiency apartment over the bookstore. All the lights in the store below were out, so I'd left the apartment door open so I could glance out the store windows to see the lightning and watch the rain streak down the windows.

Summers in Iowa can be finicky, but one thing is for certain. Rain in spring and early summer puts those of us who live on or near the Mississippi on edge. Even if we're given guarantees by meteorologists that we aren't going to get torrential rainfalls, we're wary. We've all lived through a flood or two and know the devastation one can cause. A little rainfall can quickly turn into the Lord cleansing the earth, and the next thing you know, you've got an indoor swimming pool. Of course, one full of enough bacteria to kill a herd of elephants, so it's useless, but it's there. When the "pool" recedes, you're left with enough Mississippi mud to actually build a hut or two.

Surprisingly, as much anxiety as spring and summer rains can cause, Iowans are also obsessed with summer storms. When a rainstorm—especially one accompanied by lightning flashes and ear-splitting thunder—rolls through, you'll find most of us staring out the windows or, preferably, sitting on a covered porch or enclosed patio. So, it wasn't all that strange for me to be standing on the balcony of the dark bookstore, watching the rain and flashes of blue-white light from the storm. The fact that I was in my jammies and brushing my teeth was odd, but everything else was typical.

After my teeth were thoroughly scrubbed, I held my toothbrush at my side and found myself staring hypnotically out of the bookstore windows at the rain. There was certainly something wrong with us Iowans. I shook my head to clear my thoughts and slipped back into my apartment to the bathroom. I'd barely spat out the toothpaste and rinsed my brush when the odd thundering sounds reached my ears.

Stepping into the doorway of the bathroom to listen, I glanced over to see that Rattlesnatches' ears were perked up. He was staring at the open door of the apartment, his head cocked to the side. Quickly, I returned my toothbrush to its holder, slapped the light to bathroom, and headed to the apartment door to investigate the noise. Always one step ahead, Rattlesnatches leapt from the bed and darted around me and out onto the balcony. Before I could even get to the steps leading down into the store, he had disappeared down them into the darkness.

Padding down the stairs in my bare feet, I felt like my ears had pricked up as Rattlesnatches' had been moments before. At the bottom of the stairs, I heard the thunder-like noise once again and jumped. It was knocking. Not thunder. My eyes darted to the front door of the shop and found a dark figure standing outside, cowering against the door. I raced over to the door and slapped the light switch, and the bookstore immediately flooded with light.

The rain continued to fall outside and the lightning continued to streak through the sky as thunder clapped. However, I could now easily see the man standing on the stoop of the bookstore. With wide eyes, I flipped the lock and quickly opened the door. A cool rush of wind and mist blew through the door as the man ducked inside, grumbling and fussing, wheeling a piece of luggage behind him. As soon as he was inside, I closed the door once more, blocking out the mist from the rain and the angry wind.

Though it wasn't the most welcoming thing I could think of to say, I asked the obvious question.

"What are you doing here?" I asked. "You're early!"

The man, clad in dark jeans, stylish sneakers, an expensive looking button-down, and a hooded black raincoat straightened up.

"*Really* early," I said.

Throwing back his hood, water droplets spraying the door behind him, the man finally allowed me to look at him fully. Taylor C. Tomlin was standing before me in all of his glory. All of his *annoyed, rain-soaked* glory. Even with the hood, his full head of silky black hair looked soaked. Plastered to his head and dripping into his face, it gave him the appearance of a drowned rat.

When I'd begun the organization of Head Rock Harbor's first ever Pride Weekend, I'd realized that having an LGBTQ+ author do a reading and signing at the bookstore would be a great idea. Harrison Garner, being the best-selling author of the *Detective Randy Melton Mystery series* would have made everyone in Head Rock Harbor fall all over themselves. However, the fact that *I* was Harrison Garner—*and no one except my agent and publisher knew it*—made that impossible.

So, I'd contacted my publisher and asked if there were any other LGBTQ+ authors who might be willing to come to Head Rock Harbor Books to do a reading and signing. Through a stroke of luck, they found that Taylor C. Tomlin was willing. A writer whose recent debut LGBTQ+ Young Adult book had done fair numbers, Taylor C. Tomlin could easily become the Next Big Thing. He wrote about queer kids in high school and monsters living amongst humans that only the queer kids could see and fight. An obvious and lazy metaphor for sure, but that didn't make the books any less popular.

Though Harrison Garner outsold Taylor C. Tomlin ten-to-one at Head Rock Harbor Books, Taylor still had a solid fanbase in our town. The kids at the local high school would reliably come in from time to time to buy a copy. Even the non-LGBTQ+ kids enjoyed the monster stories, even if they couldn't connect with the main characters' sexual orientations. All in all, I appreciated Taylor's book since it seemed to appeal to a broad audience but also provided representation for our community.

Standing before me, even soaked to the bone, I could see why Taylor was so popular. While I found his books fun, though nothing extraordinary, he had the look that gave him an edge over writers who wrote similar stories. With his tall stature, handsome, yet delicate features, flop of black hair, button nose, and perfect, pearly white smile, he was an easy sell. Even if you weren't completely sold on his stories, I could see the man easily getting people to buy his books.

I suddenly realized that my vintage high school t-shirt emblazoned with our school name and a silhouette of a cat— *Go Head Rock Harbor Bobcats!*—and my Woody Woodpecker jammie pants looked pretty shabby. The fact that I was barefoot, my curls were surely frizzing from the humidity and electricity in the air, and it was possible I hadn't wiped the toothpaste thoroughly from my mouth didn't help. Fighting the impulse to tug at the imaginary lapels of a nonexistent robe, I stood before Taylor, wondering if the man knew how to speak.

"Didn't my publisher tell you I was arriving early?" he asked, staring at me blankly.

I stared at him for a moment.

"They said you'd arrive Friday," I said simply.

Glowering, though not particularly at me, Taylor grumbled incomprehensibly.

"I told them I was going to be here Monday evening and that I was going to use the days leading up to this little *Pride event* to work on my next book," he said. "I'd been assured that they'd relayed the information to *you*."

Thinking about this predicament for a moment, and wondering what to do with Taylor, another obvious question came to mind.

"Why would they tell me?" I asked.

Though I'd booked him to do a reading and signing at the bookstore on the final day of Pride, it occurred to me that what Taylor did with his time before then was really none of my concern. Him arriving in town early to stay and work on his book had nothing to do with me. Meeting with Taylor the weekend of Pride, going over the schedule, and then hosting him at the bookstore for the event should have been the extent of my interactions with the man. Having him arrive nearly a week early and insinuating that I had some responsibility to do...*what?*...for him was odd, to say the least.

Taylor threw his hands up in frustration, more water droplets being flung in every which direction. Frowning, I looked around, hoping that none of the books or other paper items in the store were going to be destroyed by Taylor's complete lack of care. Though I didn't say anything, I wanted to ask my fellow author how he had such little regard for the store and the goods within that were anything but waterproof.

"Angela—*my agent?*—said you'd be able to direct me to the Inn?" he huffed.

"Oh!" I jerked. "Oh. Sure! I can do *that*," I said. "But how did you get *here?*"

"An Uber?" Taylor responded as if I was the dumbest person in the world.

"In Head Rock Harbor?" I frowned, then had a thought. "Did you take an Uber from Dubuque?"

"Obviously," he sighed, folding his arms over his chest.

The dripping of water from his coat had slowed, but a few drops still fell from the arms of his coat as he stood before me.

"Wow," I said. "That must have been a pricey ride. Why didn't you just have them take you directly to the Inn? Are you staying there to work on your book until Sunday?"

I spoke as I strode around to the back of the check-out counter to use the landline. As I made my way behind the counter, the sound of the rain on the windows was beginning to lessen. The storm was slowly dissipating. Though I had enjoyed the ambience it provided, the Iowan anxiety in me was easing up, making me less jumpy.

As I'd been making my way behind the counter and speaking to him, Taylor had taken the opportunity to look around the store. His eyes scanned the shelves, the wood floors, counter, and stairs leading up to the balcony. He stopped for a moment to eye the new coffee bar in the back corner of the store. When he finally made a full turn and his eyes landed on me once more, he looked concerned.

"Is this where I'm going to be doing the reading and signing?" he asked.

"Well, yes," I said. "This is…this is the store. Head Rock Harbor Books."

"I thought it might be…bigger."

I shrugged. "Small town, small bookstore."

The look of concern and uncertainty on his face made me chuckle.

"Don't worry," I said. "We've sold all fifty tickets and I've given away a handful of free spots for the event. You'll definitely have a crowd."

"Fifty?" He eyed me for a moment. "I suppose that's acceptable."

Taylor's tone told me that fifty people attending one of his readings was nearly insulting. Apparently, he was accustomed to much larger crowds.

"That's about all we can fit in here without violating code," I explained calmly. "But I promise you that the crowd will be receptive and enthusiastic."

I lifted the phone from the receiver.

"Do you at least have a display of my books ready?" he sighed, lowering his arms to his side.

I jabbed the phone towards the front window.

"Front window if you want to check it out," I said. "I'm going to give the Inn a call and make sure Lila is still there to check you in."

Taylor stared at me for a moment, obviously concerned that the front desk of the Inn would be closed for the evening. Of course, I was simply calling Lila to make sure she wasn't napping in the office and would be up and ready to check Taylor into his room. Though I'd only spent a few minutes with the man, getting him out of my shop and into the Inn where he could tuck away and work on his book was priority one. I could already tell that dealing with him on Sunday would be enough for me.

As I dialed up the Inn, Taylor wandered over to the front window to check out the display of his books. Though I'd arranged a nice display of more than twenty copies of his book—in case there was anyone at his event that hadn't purchased a copy yet—and had hung a temporary promotional poster in the front window, I'd already gleaned from Taylor that it would be insufficient. Of course, there was no polite way to explain to Taylor that he was in smalltown Iowa and any expectations he had about his importance would need to be lowered.

The phone was ringing in my ear as I surreptitiously watched Taylor out of the corner of my eye. He was having a hard time disguising his complete disgust with the situation he'd found himself in after arriving in Head Rock Harbor. Whether or not he was someone who would actually try to hide his feelings was another matter. From what I'd observed so far, I was certain that he was not only comfortable expressing his displeasure at anything that challenged his ego, but was accustomed to others enduring it.

"*Head Rock Harbor Inn.*" I jumped at the sound of Lila's voice suddenly pouring through the phone. "*How may I help you?*"

"Lila?" I responded, drawing Taylor's attention from across the bookstore. "It's Jackson."

"*Well, hey, Jackson,*" Lila responded, cheerful, yet confused. "*What can I do for you so late in the evening?*"

I chuckled. "Yeah. I should be in bed."

Over by the window, Taylor snorted derisively, though I felt as though he assumed I wouldn't hear.

"Taylor C. Tomlin is here," I explained, ignoring him. "He's supposed to have a reservation at the Inn? I was just checking to make sure he was set and we could get him over there to check in."

Lila was mumbling incoherently on her end of the line as I waited and Taylor stared at me. After a moment, she finally spoke into the phone.

"*He's not supposed to be here until Friday,*" Lila said, and I could hear the frustration in her voice. "*What's he doing here four days early?*"

Fortunately, before I could think of a way to respond politely with Taylor listening in, Lila began speaking again.

"*I got a room,*" she said. "*I can get him in tonight. I'll just change his reservation from Friday afternoon until Monday morning to Monday night through Monday morning. I have his publisher's payment information, so I'll just charge them. If they got a problem, they can take it up with Taylor himself.*"

Chuckling nervously, I responded, "Sounds great, Lila. Taylor will be over shortly. Thanks!"

Frowning to myself, I lowered the phone to the base. A publisher paying for an author's hotel wasn't completely unheard of, but Taylor's publisher paying for his hotel should have been. If you were an author who sold like Stephen King, a publisher would gladly shell out for a hotel bill here or there—or maybe often. However, Taylor C. Tomlin did not strike me as having sold enough books, nor was he famous enough, to have his publisher pay for a weeklong stay at a hotel. Even an inexpensive one like the Head Rock Harbor Inn.

Realizing that was none of my business, I looked up to tell Taylor what I'd gleaned from my conversation with Lila. Finding him suddenly standing on the other side of the check-out counter, I jumped again, putting a hand to my chest. The storm had certainly gotten my anxiety up.

"Sorry," I chuckled nervously. "I didn't see you walk over."

Taylor raised an annoyed eyebrow.

"Um, anyway," I said, "Lila Westbrook—the owner of Head Rock Harbor Inn—will be waiting on you. She said she'll just change your reservation from tonight until

Monday morning. She should be able to get you checked in quickly once you get there."

Satisfied with the job I'd done and the delivery of the news, I smiled at Taylor.

He stared back.

"So," I said slowly, "do you need the address? Your Uber can probably just put it into the GPS, but it's only a few blocks away and—"

"My Uber is gone!" Taylore exclaimed, his hands flying into the air once again. "How am I supposed to get there? I didn't have the car *wait* for me!"

I stopped myself before I asked the obvious question: *Why not?* Did Taylor think that showing up to the bookstore six days early for his event put me in charge of his care? Watching him as he aggressively crossed his arms over his chest again and glower at me, I realized that he actually did expect me to take care of him. Obviously, this was a man who was used to being coddled. I was beginning to wonder how'd he'd managed to hire an Uber and get it to bring him all the way to Head Rock Harbor from Dubuque on a rainy Monday night.

I had to stop myself from grinning wickedly at the thought of the Uber driver getting tired of his attitude halfway between the two and dumping him on the side of the road. As much as I had not enjoyed the few moments I'd had with the man, I could only imagine putting up with him for an entire half-hour car ride. Of course, Taylor was probably the type to ignore someone who he felt was beneath him, such as an Uber driver. Unlike me, the driver had probably had the luxury of not speaking with Taylor much.

"Well," I said finally, "if you can give me a moment, I can put on some shoes and drive you over to the Inn."

Taylor rolled his eyes. "Just…where am I going?"

Taking a breath to keep myself from telling Taylor his destination was several miles beneath us if he wanted to go there, I forced a smile onto my face.

"It's two blocks that way," I jabbed a thumb westerly, then pointed south, "and three blocks that way. Two-minute walk, tops."

I wish it was still raining, I thought to myself.

Without another word, Taylor marched over to his luggage by the front door and pulled the handle out angrily. Before I could say anything—which was probably a good thing—Taylor had ripped the front door open and had marched out into the cool night, his suitcase bouncing behind him on its wheels. Though he'd attempted to shut the door behind himself, he'd failed. The door bounced back and squeaked open a few inches. Shaking my head, I rounded the check-out counter and strolled over to shut the door.

Flipping the lock, I stared out the window and watched Taylor disappear down the street. Though I had already decided I did not like the man, and that Sunday night couldn't come and go quickly enough, I felt bad. Arriving in a strange town in the middle of a rainstorm and finding out your publisher hadn't relayed pertinent information to the person you assumed was waiting for you had to be annoying. Maybe, in the light of day, and after a good night's rest, Taylor C. Tomlin would be an entirely different person. I wasn't placing any bets, but a little hope didn't hurt.

A sudden "thump" behind me had me jumping for the third time that night. Spinning around, my eyes darted around the bookstore to find the source of the noise. Scanning the store, my eyes finally landed on the book laying at the end of one of the aisles, splayed open, text down. My eyes ran up the bookshelf until they landed on Rattlesnatches sitting at the top regally, staring down at me. I walked over to the bookshelf and squatted to pick up the book.

Monster High by Taylor C. Tomlin was the book Rattlesnatches had pushed from one of the rows in the LGBTQ+ section. I held the book in my hand and stared up at my cat. Not an ounce of remorse registered on his face, which made me smile.

"Yeah," I said as I reached up to reshelve the book, "that's pretty much how I feel about him, too."

Meow. Rattlesnatches agreed.

"Maybe he'll be better in the morning," I said with a shrug. "Come on. Let's get to bed."

By the time I'd gone over to lock the door and turn off the lights, I could hear Rattlesnatches going up the stairs like a herd of buffalo. After another quick glance out to make sure that Taylor wasn't marching back to the bookstore for further explanation or directions, I turned around. A minute later, all of the lights in the apartment were off and I was sliding under the covers as Rattlesnatches curled up next to my feet at the foot of the bed.

Chapter Six

"Close that door!" Lila Westbrook waved her hand frantically as I stepped into the lobby of the Head Rock Harbor Inn. "Quick!"

Lila's frenzied command had me hurriedly turning and shutting the front door of the Inn, then spinning around to see what had gotten her so flustered. The lobby of the Inn was empty, save the two of us, so I was confused by her demand. However, as a fellow business owner, I knew that following Lila's wishes—no matter how unusual—was best. Still startled, I approached the counter to speak with her.

"Is everything okay?" I asked, glancing around anxiously.

"Oh, honey, yes." Lila waved me off, suddenly placid. "It's just that when I opened my door this morning to walk over here to the office, I wasn't sure if I was going outside or checking the cornbread!"

A sudden realization washed over me and I met Lila's eyes. We both laughed.

"It's crazy how much hotter it is today compared to yesterday." I agreed. "That storm brought in summer."

"And I don't want you letting out all the conditioned air!" Lila cackled.

Knowing that the higher temperature was all that had bothered Lila was comforting. Though I'd done my best to slough the feeling, I was still shaken from what I'd seen at the crime scene the day before and Taylor C. Tomlin's arrival during the storm. Showing up the Head Rock Harbor Inn to another crisis would have sent me around the bend. If I had my way, I was going to avoid any sort of drama for as long as I could. With Pride Weekend coming, I knew there'd be plenty of excitement in store. Saving up my energy for that was all I wanted to focus on for the week.

"What can I do you for, Jackson?" Lila, asked, bracing her hands on the counter before leaning in conspiratorially.

"Oh, I was just checking to make sure you had your flyer up in the window, if you had any questions about this coming weekend, if you need help…those kinds of things," I said. "I guess, since I'm the de facto chief of this operation, it's my duty to make sure all the other business owners who are participating are doing okay."

Lila waved me off again.

"We're fine," she said, dismissively. "In fact, we're all booked up through next week."

"That's great!" I exclaimed.

"It's the Pride," Lila said.

Internally, I chuckled at her phrasing.

"All these young men and women coming from all over the state for it," Lila said. "I'm not so sure about some of their fashion and hairstyle choices, but their credit cards clear like anyone else's, so…"

"Well, that's good. I'm glad my people are supporting your business."

"As far as I'm concerned, you can plan events every week for us."

"Glad to hear it," I said. "Well, since you're in order, I guess I'll head on to my next stop."

"Where you off to now?" Lila asked as I shuffled towards the door again.

Stopping, my hand on the doorknob, I said, "I'm going back up to Harbor Street. I'm going to hit everything by the bookstore on my way to Munchies for lunch."

Lila smiled.

"I'll probably hit up Bernie's and a few other places after work today," I added.

Her smile was briefly replaced by a grimace, but Lila tried to recover before I noticed. Being the observant busybody that I was, I hadn't missed the look. Neither Lila nor I tried to pretend she had fooled me.

"What?" I asked.

"Well," Lila sighed, her hands falling to her sides, "just don't expect everyone to be as happy as me. That's all I'm saying and you didn't hear me say it."

"What else do you have to say that I'll have to pretend I didn't hear?" I asked, crossing my arms over my chest.

Instinctively, I'd known that not everyone would be happy about a weekend of Pride festivities in Head Rock Harbor when I agreed to organize it. However, I didn't exactly want to know which of my fellow citizens had homophobic leanings. That made it hard to frequent their businesses—or even pretend to be friends. It's difficult to be friendly with those who disagree with your very existence.

"It's not *Pride*." Lila seemed to read my mind. "I don't think anyone cares about all that."

She waved her hand in the air dismissively. My arms loosened across my chest marginally.

"But not everyone cares about tourism," Lila explained, placing her hands on the counter. "It's not just Charlene's personality that keeps people from joining her little club."

Charlene Hardy, the president of the Harbor Street Business Owners' Association, had been trying to get all of us to join her "club" for months. So far, she had been unsuccessful. One, Harbor Street really didn't have enough businesses to warrant an association. Two, no one really liked to spend more time with Charlene Hardy than was necessary. And I couldn't blame them. After getting involved with the murder investigation of Prescott Pemberton in late spring due to her insistence I help her with the sale of his house for his family, I tried to avoid her even more.

"What do you mean?" I asked.

"Some folks have been around here since Moses was drifting down the river," Lila said. "They don't like the council, Linda, and Charlene trying to stir up tourism. They want things to stay the way they are."

"Well, Linda is the mayor," I said. "It's her job to help the local economy. Same for the council."

I had no excuse for Charlene.

"Sure, sure," Lila said dismissively. "But the older folks around here can get feisty about it. That's all. Some of them aren't looking forward to all the out of towners coming in and causing all the noise for a weekend. I was over at Bernie's the other night. Just to see my cousin, mind you."

"Who goes to Bernie's and why is none of my business," I said.

Lila grinned impishly. "And he was fussing about some college kids who'd come in and called his place a *dive bar* before asking for some fancy cocktails and beers he'd never even heard of before. He said he gave them all a Pabst, wouldn't let them start a tab, and hurried them out after they'd finished their drink. Sent them all off to your mother's place."

I couldn't help but laugh. Bernie forcing fancy college kids to drink PBR and then leave sounded exactly like him.

Lila chuckled. "Folks just don't take to people from out of town trying to make us something we're not."

"I get it," I said. "I really do. But it's just one weekend. None of these folks are going to come here for Pride and then start looking at real estate. I assure you."

Who'd want to move to Head Rock Harbor? I thought. *We don't even have a movie theater.*

For entertainment in our little town, you had to be happy with drinking yourself to death, spending time with the Lord, eating greasy food, or mucking it up on the river. If you wanted anything actually fun to do, you had to drive up to Dubuque. A thirty-minute drive to catch the latest Marvel movie was not ideal to most—especially if they hadn't grown up with that reality.

"Well, them fellas bought up The Downtown!" Lila exclaimed. "And they bought Ona Evans' old place!"

"The Downtown," I used the shortened version of the theater's name to match Lila's energy, "had been boarded up since I was a baby."

"Well—"

"And Ona Evans' old place had been collecting weeds, broken windows, teenagers' beer cans—*and other used items*—since my mother was in high school," I said. "Randall and Michael are going to remodel them and get rid of two eyesores, Lila. And we'll have a theater again!"

"*Live* theater," she said, rolling her eyes. "Culture!"

I laughed uproariously, and she joined me.

"We need a *real* theater," she said. "We all want to see the latest movie, not Hamlet!"

"I don't think Shakespeare is what they have in mind," I said to reassure her. "I think it'll be live shows that appeal to…the town. Besides, what can I say? Streaming killed the movie house."

"We'll see," Lila squinted at me. "We'll see."

Obviously, Lila had missed my 80s pop reference.

"By the way," I began, "sorry about the late-night call last night. Did Taylor get checked in okay?"

Lila rolled her eyes and breath gushed from her mouth in exasperation.

"That's a fussy one," she said, shaking her head. "Wanted our *best room* and *lots of clean towels* and wanted to know if I could send him up a pot of hot tea. Like this is the Ritz or something!"

Laughing, I couldn't help but feel a little guilty. I wasn't entirely responsible for Taylor's behavior, but Head Rock Harbor Books—and Pride—were the reasons for him being in town. He wouldn't have ever known about Head Rock Harbor Inn or darkened Lila's doorstep if it wasn't for me.

"I had plenty of towels, of course, and I managed to find him some hot water and some tea bags," Lila sniffed. "I don't think it was to his standards, though."

"He definitely seems...particular." I agreed. "Hopefully, he'll stay up in his room writing until Sunday night and then Monday morning he'll be a memory."

She laughed. "Well, as long as he leaves here never wanting to come back, it'll be okay. I'll make sure he doesn't have too nice a time. We don't want him reporting that this is the best place on earth."

I shook my head and reached for the doorknob again.

"Well, I'm telling you, it'll be all right. Head Rock Harbor is not in danger of a population boom anytime soon. At least, not in a timeframe that should concern you or Bernie."

Lila gasped. "I am not that old!"

We both laughed again. With a nod and a wink, I exited the Head Rock Harbor Inn, closing the door quickly and tightly behind me, saving as much *conditioned air* as possible. Swiftly, I made my way back up to Harbor Street, but I didn't stop at any other businesses once there. Having a handful of discussions similar to the one I'd just had with Lila was out of the question. I'd never get to lunch and back to the bookstore to reopen for the day if I did.

Five minutes after leaving the Inn, I was slipping through the front door of Munchies. It didn't immediately register with me as I scanned the small dining room for Jeremy, but something was off about the lunch crowd. Typically, Lardell and Shirley turned more than a few tables during the lunch rush on week days at Munchies. Without taking time to count, I could tell that the dining room felt busier than most days.

After spotting Jeremy in our usual booth in the back corner, I made my way through the restaurant. A few creatively dressed and coiffed diners stood out in the corner of my eye as I walked over to join him. When I passed behind Shirley as she waited on one such group of folks, I nearly tripped over my own feet at their conversation.

"*Where do you source your eggs?*" a young man asked her.

"*From the Hy-Vee.*" Shirley's deadpan reply followed.

Trying not to laugh, I finished my walk to the booth and slid in across from Jeremy. He eyed me as I settled into the booth and grabbed a menu from the holder at the end of the table. Over the years I'd been dining at Munchies, I'd memorized the menu, and I almost always ordered the same thing. Pork tenderloin, fries, and coleslaw. However, I operated under the assumption that Lardell might sneak some new, tastier dish onto the menu, and I would have to try it.

A quick glance had told me I was wrong.

"Unique crowd today," Jeremy said quietly as I slid the menu back into the holder.

"I'm going to be run out of town on a rail," I replied.

Jeremy's eyebrow rose and the corner of his mouth quirked up.

"That could be fun," he said.

"Don't be a pervert."

"It's in my DNA," he said with a shrug. "But, for the sake of conversation, why are you going to be run out of town?"

"All the tourists," I leaned in to whisper. "They're everywhere this week. It was only supposed to be for a weekend. And, apparently, they're annoying people."

Jeremy thought about that.

"Well, we have had trouble keeping them away from the sandbar. Getting them to understand it's an active crime scene—and trying to keep it quiet—is like explaining physics to a toddler."

I held my hands out in a "see what I mean" kind of gesture.

"But I don't think the town blames you, Jacks."

"I don't know. Lila Westbrook told me a few people had things to say about all of the tourists."

"Lila Westbrook and all the other old fogies in this town always find something to be crotchety about," Jeremy said. "Don't let it get to you."

Though I'd had a response loaded, planning to inform Jeremy that the older people in town had opinions that mattered, I was forced to drop it. Shirley arrived at our table to take our order. By the time I'd informed her that I was going to be eating my usual, and Jeremy had rattled off his order, the point was lost. Telling Jeremy that the City Council and Linda Wagner—and his boss, *the police chief*—might actually care about the older citizens' opinions was moot. Jeremy was as aware of the social structure of Head Rock Harbor as I.

Since I'd decided that harping on the current influx of tourists was pointless, my brain shifted gears. I hadn't texted Jeremy the day before and asked him out to lunch to discuss tourism anyway. There was another pressing matter that I needed to go over with my best friend.

"So," I said, "you're probably wondering why I asked you out to lunch."

"You missed looking at this handsome face?" Jeremy leaned forward, positively cherubic as he batted his eyes comically.

I stared at him for a moment, and when he realized I wasn't going to banter, he sat back and slumped in the booth. Preparing to tear into my best friend about nosing in on my business the day before, I cleared my throat and leaned forward, laying my arms on the tabletop. Before I could chastise Jeremy for eavesdropping on my call, he spoke again.

"I guess I was hoping that you missed hanging out with me as much as I've missed hanging out with you over the last month," Jeremy said suddenly. "I know you've been busy and all—and work hasn't been a picnic for me—but I hoped that was it."

Swallowing the words that had been about to spark fire from my lips and set my friend on fire, I stared at Jeremy from across the table. Even though he had overstepped and completely invaded my privacy in my own home the day before, he'd presently stalled me. Getting onto him now, or even speaking sternly, would feel like kicking a wounded puppy. The way he sat back in the booth and stared down at his hands clasped in his lap, all I could feel was guilty.

I had been ignoring him for a month.

"Well, it does go both ways," I said.

I wasn't going to kick him when he was down, but I certainly wasn't going to take all of the blame for our month of self-imposed separation.

"True," Jeremy said, nodding. "I'm not blaming you. I'm not blaming me. I'm blaming us."

"We've been busy. As you said."

He nodded. "Always busy."

We both knew that we were tiptoeing around the elephant in the room like a pair of mice afraid of startling it and getting stomped.

"Listen," I said, not wanting any weirdness between us, "Deacon and I—"

"You are allowed to do whomever and whatever you want," Jeremy held his hands up. "You don't owe me anything."

"*I'm not doing anyone right now*," I mumbled, mostly to myself, but Jeremy caught it and smirked. "That's not the point. When you took me back to the bookstore that morning and…well…*you know*…I'm still…*thinking*…about that."

Jeremy raised an eyebrow and began to speak, but Shirley chose that moment to arrive with our plates of food. As she set my pork tenderloin, fries, and coleslaw in front of me, and a giant BLT with house made chips in front of Jeremy, I looked up to find her eyeing me.

"What?" I asked.

"*This is your fault*," she leaned in to whisper, though the words were delivered with a smile.

She glanced over her shoulder furtively at one of the tables full of queer hipsters behind her. Shrinking in my booth seat, my cheeks felt hot. Shirley chuckled and reached out to give my shoulder a quick squeeze.

"We're making money over fist," she said as a way to ease the guilt. "Don't worry about it."

Jeremy chuckled evilly as Shirley ruffled my hair and began to walk away. As she turned, I heard her mumble, *'where do we source our eggs?'* with all the incredulity she could muster. Sighing to myself, I retrieved my fork from the roll of utensils in the paper napkin and zeroed in on my slaw. Jeremy was shaking the ketchup bottle as he stared at me from across the table.

"So," he said as my fork slid into the bowl of slaw, "thinking what exactly?"

Pausing for a moment, I wasn't certain I wanted, or was ready, to have a full-blown conversation about the kiss Jeremy had plastered on me after we'd solved Carter Nelson's non-murder. Or his invitation to "come hang out" at his place for the day. Obviously, we'd eventually have to discuss the event and invitation, and where exactly Jeremy thought following through with his invitation would lead us. Having the conversation so soon wasn't something I was certain I wanted, though.

"Just thinking," I said before stuffing a forkful of slaw in my mouth.

Chewing and looking down at my food nonchalantly, I hoped that Jeremy would let the topic die off and we could move on to something less uncomfortable. Like gall bladder surgery or intimate warts. I knew my best friend well enough to know that I wasn't going to luck out.

"Jacks," Jeremy said, "I told you whatever you needed."

"Yeah?"

"And I meant it," he said with a sigh. "I don't like it, but I mean it. You can *think* about whatever you need to think about, however you need to think about it. With whoever you need to think about it with. I put you on the spot with the kiss."

"It was kind of a shock," I said. "And it's *whomever*."

Jeremy chuckled pitifully. "*Irregardless*, I'm a man of my word. You just...think. All right? But let's not avoid each other. Deal?"

"Deal," I said. "And you just had to say 'irregardless', didn't you?"

Jeremy waggled his head and stuck out his tongue. Laughing, I dug into my coleslaw again, and within a minute, the bowl was empty. Jeremy attacked his food with the same ravenous abandon, and within a few minutes of feral chowing on both of our parts, our plates were nearly empty. Though we weren't avoiding talking to each other, it's impossible to carry on a conversation when your jaws are full of the delicious food Lardell cooks. So, we ate in amiable silence, only the animalistic sounds of our teeth gnashing as our soundtrack.

As I was leaning back in my booth and patting my stomach discreetly, Jeremy plucked a stray crumble of bacon off of his plate that had somehow managed to escape his sandwich. Popping the piece into his mouth happily, his phone dinged. Jeremy slid his phone out of his hip pocket and swiped to unlock it. I grabbed the check from the table and popped the last two fries on my plate into my mouth.

"Oh, boy," Jeremy snorted.

"What is it?" I asked as I smiled down at the ticket that said '*on the house*'.

Crumpling up the ticket and placing it on my plate, Jeremy shook his head and looked up at me from his phone.

"I've been summoned back to the PD for a meeting," he said.

"Oof."

"With Marv. *And Linda.*"

Frowning, I said, "You have to meet with the chief and the mayor? Why?"

Leaning in, Jeremy gave me a look as if I was dense.

"The murder at the sandbar, maybe?" he replied.

I made a mocking face and started to slide out of the booth. If Jeremy had to go back to the police department, lunch was officially over. Going back to the bookstore and opening up for the rest of the day was my plan.

"Hold up, hot shot," Jeremy said with a chuckle.

"What?" I asked, pausing.

"Your presence is requested at this meeting," Jeremy said, smiling wickedly. "Marv knew I was at lunch with you."

"I can't be summoned to a meeting." I scoffed. "I don't work for the police department. Or the city."

Jeremy shrugged. "Don't come with me then. If you want Marv and Linda to march into the bookstore in ten minutes."

Grumbling, I slid out of the booth and stood at the tableside to look down at Jeremy.

"Can I at least get a ride?" I asked.

Jeremy grinned.

"To the PD," I mumbled, my face feeling hot.

"Of course," Jeremy slid out of the booth and rose to look down at me. "Let's roll."

Chapter Seven

Officer Riley was behind his desk per usual and I'd taken up a seat in one of the uncomfortable plastic chairs by the front door. Assuming I was the least important—and invested—person at this impromptu meeting, I hoped to be forgotten if I stayed out of the way. Jeremy was sitting on his desk, his hands gripping the edge, as his feet dangled. My hands were folded in my lap and I watched as Chief Marvin Bucksworth paced back and forth and Mayor Linda Wagner stood rigid in the middle of the room, her arms crossed over her chest. Her husband, Mark, was doing his best to look small in the corner of the front office.

"So," Marv began as we all listened, "since the police department, the mayor's office, and you, Jackson, are the leaders in this Pride Weekend event, we need to be on the same page."

Folding my arms over my chest, I sat back and stared at Marv, my eyes following him as he paced back forth across the room. Linda was alternating between watching Marv pace and glancing over at me as I watched him.

"Though it's rare that the news takes any interest in our little town," Marv continued, "we have to expect that it's possible we'll get a few local stations coming to town over the weekend. We don't expect that any will show up on Friday and stay for the weekend, or if they'll even pop up at all. But if they do, it'll because they'll want to come into town to report on *the little river town embracing diversity and inclusion* and all of that noise."

I couldn't argue with Marv's assessment. Local Iowa news stations loved reporting on such things.

"Make their little three-minute human interest pieces for the eleven o'clock news and whatnot," Marv explained further. "Certainly, they'll be ambushing the out-of-towners who are here for Pride and river activities."

Nodding, I still had nothing to disagree with in Marv's speech.

"However, without a doubt, they're going to want a sound bite from Mayor Wagner," Marv said, gesturing at Linda, "any City Council members they can find, me, and local business owners who are participating in events."

"Sure," I said.

Jeremy and Officer Riley were nodding along. Mark was still cowering in the corner. The poor man had been married to Linda for two decades. If he made it to a quarter century, I'd eat my hat.

"Obviously," Marv stopped pacing and sighed, looking at me, "they're also going to want to talk to the man who organized the entire thing."

My throat felt like a mild acid was bubbling up.

"That's you," Marv said, as though we weren't all clear on what he'd been implying. "And we want to make sure that Pride is the *only* thing that gets discussed."

Frowning so deeply that a canyon was cutting through my brow, I stared at Marv. Glancing over at Linda, then Jeremy, I couldn't help but be confused.

"Okay?" I asked.

Marv grumbled under his breath.

"We don't want any mention of the incident at the sandbar," Marv said. "There's no reason for the Pride Weekend news pieces to include mention of any deaths."

My face went blank and I folded my arms over my chest tightly.

"We can't help it if anyone whispers something to reporters about the incident," Marv was pacing again, "but we don't want to encourage any of them to focus on *that* instead of Pride."

"The murder, you mean?" I asked.

Marv stopped pacing and turned to glare at me. Linda's stance became more rigid.

"Jackson," Linda jumped in before Marv could respond, "we don't want all of your hard work and the time, energy, and money spent by the city and its business owners to be for naught."

I cocked an eyebrow as I turned my head to stare at her.

"If and when a reporter approaches you," Linda said, dread at the prospect of me being interviewed lacing her tone, "let's make sure everything you have to say is about your hard work in organizing this event for Head Rock Harbor. Nothing about the incident."

"Murder," I said again.

Linda and Marv exchanged a glance.

"A man was killed. He's not an *incident*," I said.

Out of the corner of my eye, I saw Jeremy doing his best to keep a neutral expression. Though the topic was grave, I knew he wanted to laugh at my refusal to play nice with Marv and Linda.

"We're aware that this event was tragic," Linda said, speaking for both her and Marv again. "However, there is still the matter of what is at stake if out-of-towners are scared off, or a reporter decides to paint our town in a certain light. I'm sure we can all agree that focusing on what a wonderful event Pride is for our town is what matters."

"And we want to make sure that all the money put into it isn't wasted," Marv added.

Staring at the both of them, I was struck dumb by the fact that we'd all been summoned to the police department for an impromptu meeting. One that seemed, specifically, to be about telling me to stay in line. Marv and Linda had gotten it into their heads that I was a loose cannon who was going to put on a tin foil hat, jump in front of a news camera and speak tongues about dead bodies and murderers on the loose.

Gloria's voice was carrying down the hall in our silence. Apparently, things being slow, as they usually were in Head Rock Harbor when no one was actively being killed, she was using he free time to discuss roast chicken recipes with a friend. I let the seconds tick by uncomfortably as Linda and Marv stared at me, practically wringing their hands as they waited for me to respond.

"I'm not sure why you think I'm eager to be interviewed by anyone, let alone a reporter," I said finally. "I'm just trying to get through this week, the weekend, and move on with my plans for the bookstore. If I can avoid being interviewed, that's the plan. In fact, I plan to avoid tourists as much as possible, aside from actual planned events or selling them books."

Linda and Marv seemed to relax marginally.

"But if you're so worried about the *murder* and Pride Weekend coinciding, there's always the option of cancelling everything," I suggested. "We can revisit the idea of a Pride Weekend next year."

Linda's hand went to her chest and she looked as though she'd gotten a sudden case of the vapors. Marv, even more dramatically, marched over behind his desk, and flopped into his chair like a rag doll. Jeremy was in the corner of my eye, rubbing at his mouth as if grins could be rubbed off.

"Did you not hear Marv talking about the money?" Linda exhaled heavily. "Business owners—*your friends*—have spent money. *Your mother* has spent money. If we cancel everything it was all wasted for them. Do you want that, Jackson?"

"Well, no, but—"

"Then why would you even suggest such a thing?" Linda gasped.

Mark was practically shivering like a frightened chihuahua in the corner. I nearly had to rub a smile off my face, but managed to control myself.

"Just a thought," I shrugged. "You and Marv seem a little high strung about everything. Just trying to be helpful. If you're that worried, it's an option. That's all."

"It is *not* an option," Linda demanded, pointing a witchy-poo finger at me.

"Not at all," Marv enunciated each word.

I looked around the room at the three other men, hoping any of them would at least say that I wasn't being unreasonable. Surprisingly, Officer Riley spoke up.

"Jackson isn't wrong," he said, twirling lazily in his chair. "It's not a bad idea if you think there'll be a problem. Especially since we don't know who the victim is, who did it, or if they're still around. Put out a notice that due to unforeseen circumstances and whatnot."

"We don't want it to happen to someone else," Jeremy agreed.

I started to smile.

"Then again," Jeremy continued, "canceling everything could embolden a violent person—if they're still hanging around, that is."

My smile was gone in an instant. Jeremy gave me an apologetic look as he continued.

"It's known that violent people are often encouraged into further violence if they see that they have any kind of power—such as getting an entire city to cancel events out of fear," Jeremy said. "Sorry, Jacks."

I ignored him.

The grins on Marv's and Linda's faces were enough to turn me off food. At least until dinner.

"Fine," I said, standing from the chair. "Pride Weekend is on. Hope it's a blood bath. Are we done here?"

Officer Riley twirled in his chair, and I caught that he had turned to hide the smile that had bloomed on his face. Jeremy was rubbing at his lips again. Linda and Marv looked absolutely defeated, but resigned to the fact that they'd gotten the best they could out of me.

"If you are approached by a reporter, you—" Linda began.

"Yeah, yeah," I waved her off as I made my way towards the door. "I'll make sure to tell them that the town is totally safe, no *incidents* have occurred, and, *hey, just for funsies, walk around in groups for safety.*"

Linda gasped. Marv threw his hands up. Mark shivered.

"If anyone needs a book, you know where I'll be," I said. As I approached the door, I added a final thought over my shoulder. "But if you had any decency, you'd at least cancel the swimming and live music at the sandbar Saturday. A guy was killed there yesterday, for crying out loud."

With that, I exited the police department, a waft of oven-like air gushing in as I dashed away. Pulling the glass door shut behind me, I marched down the sidewalk, fully intending to make my way back to the bookstore. However, it occurred to me that, as my own boss, I didn't have to do anything I didn't want to do. So, I found myself plopping down on the city bench at the corner. The metal slats were like irons, even through my jeans, causing me to shift uncomfortably until I adjusted to the heat.

As I expected would happen, Jeremy was plopping down on the bench moments later. Leaving the police department in the way that I had warranted that he check on me. The fact that he hadn't completely backed me up when I'd suggested canceling Pride meant that he was required to follow. When a best friend doesn't have your back—no matter how sound their reasoning—they are required to do their mea culpas. I don't make the rules.

The fact that Jeremy had chosen to sit so close that his hip was touching mine when there was plenty of space on the bench was not lost on me. However, I didn't give him the satisfaction of appearing to be bothered.

"That was not a meeting," I said, turning my head to glower at him. "That was an ambush."

"I didn't know," Jeremy said, reading my mind.

"You better not have," I said, warning him.

"Linda and Marv singling you out as though you're some public relations nightmare was definitely not on my mind," Jeremy said. "I thought they were going to suggest some amped up security or something for Pride. Not…what they just did."

"I don't wish what happened to that man at the sandbar on anyone, but if the person who did it is looking for more victims…"

Jeremy cough-laughed.

"I'm only kidding," I said, slumping on the bench.

"I know, I know," Jeremy said.

He laid a hand on my knee. I chose to not protest.

"I have to attend a lot of the Pride events while running a bookstore this weekend," I said with a sigh. "I have to make sure things go off without a hitch. And I have to host the second to last event of the weekend at the bookstore—a book signing with the most annoying and arrogant young adult author of all time. Who—to make this week better—decided to arrive nearly a week early."

"Huh?" Jeremy chuckled.

"Taylor C. Tomlin," I said, as if that explained a lot. "He wasn't supposed to be here until Friday. Which makes sense, right?"

Jeremy nodded.

"He arrived last night," I explained. "Apparently, he wants to spend the week leading up to the book signing on Sunday working on his next manuscript at the Inn. And he is fussy."

"Fussy?"

"Well," I said, "it's just the impression that I get. Kind of arrogant. Particular about things. Annoying."

Jeremy was grinning, though I could see the pity in his eyes.

"He's not bad to look at," I said, "don't get me wrong. But beauty is only skin deep."

"Watch it," Jeremy nudged my shoulder with his. "I'll start to get jealous."

I rolled my eyes at him, but I couldn't keep the smile off my face. We sat in silence for a moment before Jeremy spoke up. His hand was still on my knee, which he gave a squeeze.

"Look," Jeremy said, "I'll level with you. I didn't know this was going to happen with Marv and Linda today. Like they were going to treat you as if you were some problem the town had to deal with, okay?"

"Fine."

"But it's clear that Linda has it in her mind that you are a problem," Jeremy said with a sigh. "And she's been trying to convince Marv of it, too."

"She's doing a good job from what I can tell," I huffed.

"Well," Jeremy said, "that's kind of my fault. After Prescott Pemberton's and Marshelle Martin's murders—and you being involved with that, I shouldn't have asked for your help with Carter Nelson's death."

I sat there, listening.

"Having you at the center of three deaths and their investigations has made it look like you're a troublemaker to Linda," Jeremy explained. "And, from her perspective, you can't blame her."

"I'll blame her all I want," I said.

Chuckling, Jeremy said, "And then you're also kind of responsible. Showing up like that on the sandbar the other day to get in business that was none of yours? Wasn't a good look to Marv, Jacks."

I opened my mouth to speak, thought about it for a second, then closed my mouth. I repeated the action enough times to look like a dying fish. Jeremy grinned at me as I did my best to come up with a decent defense.

"Well," I finally said, "if I hadn't been involved in the other three investigations—*one at your behest*—I wouldn't have felt like it was my business to show up at the sandbar."

"Fair enough," Jeremy said, not bothering to fight me, which was shocking. "But you can still see how you shouldn't have shown up, right? And how that looked to Marv?"

Grumbling, I stood from the bench, Jeremy's hand falling from my knee. Somehow, I missed the feeling of his reassuring—and possibly presumptuous—hand squeezing the joint through my jeans. However, I would never admit such a thing at such a moment.

"Oh," I grumbled, "go, solve a murder. And I'll stay out of it. Happy?"

"A bit," Jeremy said, nodding up at me.

Producing a rude hand gesture, which only made Jeremy grin wider, I spun on my heels and marched away. Jeremy had done his mea culpas. And given me a few of my own.

Chapter Eight

To say that I was in no mood to reopen the store for the rest of Tuesday was an understatement. The meeting with Linda and Marv had put me in a snit. The upcoming Pride Weekend events and the anxiety they were creating, and my thoughts on Jeremy, had me too flustered to deal with sales. In addition, if I was being completely honest with myself, the majority of my sales happened after four o'clock on weekdays and on Fridays and Saturdays. Once the coffee bar was open and Angel was pumping caffeine into the community, things might change. In the meantime, not being open on a Tuesday afternoon didn't throw my monthly ledger into chaos.

As I stared at my laptop resting under the check-out counter, I was never happier to have the income from the *Detective Randy Melton Mystery series*. The five book series—with my editor possessing the sixth manuscript— had sold more copies than I ever could have dreamed of when I began writing them. Even if I didn't sell another book in the store, I could keep the lights on for the rest of my life.

As layers of dust began to look like attic insulation on the neglected stock, I'd still have food to eat and heat when the days were cold. I wouldn't be buying a BMW or Rolex watches, but I'd never go hungry or not have a roof over my head.

Like many people, I don't want to set the world on fire, I just want to be able to pay the gas bill.

It struck me that if I hadn't chosen to write the series under the pen name Harrison Garner, the series might be even more popular. Traveling around like Taylor C. Tomlin—with a more gracious demeanor—and doing readings and signings would absolutely behoove sales. However, the fact that I was absolutely mortified at the prospect of possibly talking to the local news channels about Pride Weekend undercut that fantasy. Standing in front of rooms full of strangers and speaking, introducing myself and making small talk with person after person in a line of people waiting to have their books signed, and doing actual interviews, was a debilitating phobia.

The thought of someone asking me a question such as *how did you come up with the idea of Detective Randy Melton?*—and expecting an intelligent answer—petrified me. My power with words is on the page, not through speaking. If all interviews could possibly be done via email, fame might not be such a bad thing. Alas, the world did not cater to the perpetually introverted and socially awkward, such as myself.

Choosing to believe the mystery surrounding Harrison Garner's identity helped make the series a hit was going to be my belief for the foreseeable future.

Since my current manuscript was still with my editor—and she hadn't responded to clarify the notes she'd sent about the climax—and I wasn't opening the store for the rest of the day, I decided to devote the afternoon to hobbies. And a grumpy Abyssinian who seemed to feel that he had been neglected and abused for the previous month. I'd been so busy with Pride Weekend preparations, Rattlesnatches hadn't gotten as much daily attention as he was used to receiving.

A half-hour of kitty cat fishing pole aerobics for the second day in a row, ear scratches, and head boops was all it took to get myself back in the good graces of my feline best friend. Of course, the few tablespoons of canned tuna I'd presented to him didn't hurt, either. Once he'd had enough activities and indicated that sleeping on my lap was what he had in mind, I turned my focus to the J.R.R. Tolkien cross-stitch piece I'd been working on as time permitted over the last month. A stitched map of Middle Earth with the caption "*Not all those who wander are lost*" was a project I'd hoped to complete before the book signing with Taylor on Sunday.

Having a literary-inspired cross-stitch piece displayed at the check-out counter for the signing would delight locals and tourists alike. All of my regulars looked forward to seeing what creation I came up with next. If books and cross-stitch intersected, they'd be over the moon. However, with only half of the intricate piece completed, I'd given up the dream of having it displayed during the signing on Sunday. Even if I had nothing else to do for the next five days, it would be impossible to finish such a complex project in such a small amount of time.

That thought stuck in my craw for several minutes as I squinted down at the cross-stitch and my fingers worked the needle in and out of the squares. Knowing that Pride Weekend was coming, and feeling completely overwhelmed, it occurred to me that I could close up shop through the following Tuesday. Aside from the book signing on Sunday night, there wasn't anything forcing me to keep regular hours. Not having to worry about the income and being able to close the shop for a few days was a privilege I needed to take advantage of every once and a while.

There had been no opportunity to flex my privilege before, so there was no time like the present. Setting my cross-stitch aside, I carefully pulled my laptop up from under the counter, making sure to not disturb the slumbering cat on my lap. As Rattlesnatches snuggled into my lap, as though subconsciously dreaming of me trying to escape him, I set the laptop on the counter. Flipping it open, I brought up my graphics program to make a sign for the window. Once I had something professional and attractive designed, I'd shoot it to the printer and hang it up.

Working on the sign did not disturb Rattlesnatches' slumber one bit. As peaceful as a corpse, he napped as I swiped my fingers over the tracking pad and tapped away at the keys. One wouldn't think that making a sign for a shop window would be all that time-consuming or complicated, but I liked to keep things classy and professional at Head Rock Harbor Books. A simple printed sign telling people to show up for the book signing Sunday night and that normal hours would resume on Tuesday didn't slice the pie for me.

Writers and shopkeepers.

We'll do anything to waste time.

Or to keep ourselves from doing actual work.

Smiling to myself at the thought, I continued to work on the sign. There was nothing else for me to concentrate on for the evening, aside from the cross-stitch, so I wasn't really wasn't time. Or maybe I was and didn't want to admit it. Either way, the sign that eventually got hung in the window would at least have some pizzazz.

Halfway through the creation of the sign, my phone dinged, indicating a text was received.

Pulling my phone from my pocket and unlocking it, I found a message from Deacon. Smiling automatically, I opened the text.

I am texting you to formally request your company on a second date. Parade, Feast, and Rainbow Lights Friday? Seems fitting to have our second date on the first night of Pride. You know. The whole Gay Thing?

Chuckling, I tapped out a response.

How fortunate for you that two of those things are free and the other costs five bucks a head.

Deacon's response was quick.

I'm charming, not rich. But if charm made money, I'd be a Rockefeller.

Laughing out loud, I replied.

I've got tickets to the Pride Food and Wine Pairings at The Dock Saturday. And to the Rainbow Rave at Harper's after. Play your cards right Friday and I might invite you.

Deacon's response indicated we had a deal, and I replied in agreement. Going back to my sign, I was glad to know I had a date for a few of the Pride Weekend events. Being the organizer—and gay—I somehow felt sad that I was also single. Having Deacon to accompany me to some events would lessen the embarrassment.

By the time I'd gotten the bulk of the work done on the sign and I was messing with fonts to make everything perfect, the sun was setting outside. Golden hour light was beginning to pour through the windows, making the highly polished dark woods in the shop gleam. Unfortunately, it also accentuated the dust motes swirling through the stale air. Sighing to myself at the knowledge that more cleaning would need to be done soon, I continued working.

As I was nearly convinced that the correct font for the sign was Garamond, I was distracted from my task by the muffled squeal of tires outside. Looking up in time, I caught the black streak of Jeremy's car flying by on Harbor Street. Frowning to myself, I wondered what could possibly be important enough that he would be so reckless on a street frequented by pedestrians.

Nearly coming off the stool to go jump in my car and chase him down, I had to force myself to stay seated. Obviously, the part of my brain that wanted to be involved in police business had automatically activated—and I wasn't supposed to follow those impulses anymore. No more dead bodies. No more murders. No more butting into Jeremy's or any police business. If he was racing to the scene of another murder, that was between him, the victim, and God, as far as I was concerned. Jackson Harper was a detective in the pages and a bookseller in the streets.

Period.

However, when another muffled squeal of tires sounded, and I looked up to find one of the department's cruisers shooting off the opposite way on Harbor Street, I had to force myself to stay still. Why Jeremy was racing one way and Officer Ashley Riley—or maybe Marv—was racing off the other was a mystery that would have to stay unsolved. Thinking to myself that I could probably eventually ask Jeremy what had happened, I felt a little calmer. Once Pride Weekend was gone, things had settled down, and he was in an amenable mood, I could get all of the gossip from my best friend.

As the thought swirled through my head, Rattlesnatches started, his head jerking up, twitching around, his ears going haywire. Then he was streaking from my lap, unfortunately, using his claws to propel himself away from me. Dashing away across the counter and off into the depths of the store, he knocked over the display of Harrison Garner books on the counter. Books spilled over the front of the counter, only one landing on the actual counter. Clutching my jeans-clad thigh, I grimaced.

"Cheese and rice! Got all muddy!" I growled. *"You better run you little fuzzball!"*

Holding onto my thigh and applying pressure like a soldier who had taken grenade shrapnel, I scoured the shop with angry eyes. Whatever had gotten under Rattlesnatches' skin and sent him running away like a terror, he'd been smart enough to get out of sight. Making people bleed was one of the no-no's in our home. We hadn't had an incident in months, and I'd lulled myself into a false sense of security with my feline companion. It was obvious that the periods between maulings would grow, but the maulings would never cease completely.

After a moment, and the pain in my thigh subsiding, I realized it was time to give up on everything and make dinner. An early bedtime—or at least, getting into bed early to watch a movie—was not an entirely awful idea. I saved my work and closed my laptop before stowing it back under the check-out counter. I put away my cross-stitch and slid from the stool to clean up the toppled books.

Rattlesnatches continued to make himself scarce and quiet as I rounded the counter and retrieved the four toppled books from the floor. I had to adjust a few dustcovers—fortunately, none were torn or crinkled—before stacking the books on the counter. I laid book number five, *The Curse and the Coffin*, on the counter, spine outward so customers could easily see and read it. Atop it came the fourth, third, and second books, *An Historical Homicide, Torture at High Tea,* and *Blood in the Basement*. Finally, atop the pile I stood the first book in the series, *A Corpse in the Cabinet*. Harrison Garner was, once again, on prominent display by the register.

Remembering that I had pot stickers in the freezer and some new spicy garlic noodles I wanted to try, I found myself bounding up the stairs to my apartment moments later.

Maybe the day wasn't a total waste.

Chapter Nine

Placing the sign in the front window of the shop the next day felt like a failure and an accomplishment at the same time. Taking time off was against my nature, and I'd been planning to fix that personality defect at some point. So, randomly taking time for myself felt like an accomplishment. However, taking time off because I felt overwhelmed made the timing of the accomplishment feel like a failure. My thought processes about closing the shop for a few days would make no sense to anyone else, but it was how my brain worked.

Instead of focusing on my psychoses, I adjusted the sign in the corner of the front window, making sure it was straight, then fixed it in place with invisible tape. When any customers—especially regulars—stopped by, they'd see the sign telling them not to worry. Head Rock Harbor Books wasn't closed permanently, it was merely on hiatus in preparation for the book signing and the rest of Pride Weekend. On Tuesday, we'd be back to normal hours—*and with a new coffee bar!* The time off would be worth it to everyone!

That was the story I was going to stick with to make my brain settle down, anyway.

It occurred to me that if I was going to have the shop closed until Tuesday, and only open for the evening of the book signing, there was more information my customers needed. Rooting around under the check-out counter for the promotional package Taylor C. Tomlin's publisher had sent, I found the sign they'd included. Eleven by eighteen inches, the slick poster they'd made for Sunday's book signing needed to replace the temporary sign in the window as well.

Shaking my head at the sign, which included a glamorous black-and-white headshot of the dark-haired author, I headed back over to the window. Using invisible tape once again, I hung the signage next to the display of Taylor's books in the front window and removed the temporary sign. Advertising the date and time of the book signing for Sunday, along with "fun" facts about the author next to his picture, the sign would surely inform my customers of anything they needed to know. And Tayor couldn't say that I hadn't used any of the materials provided by his publisher.

As I finished hanging the sign, it occurred to me that I would need to let Angel know about the store being closed until Tuesday. If he stopped by to discuss his new job and duties and saw the sign, he might feel slighted that I hadn't told him about it directly. Telling Taylor about the store being closed until the book signing was also paramount. If he stopped by the store for any reason and saw that I wasn't in and the store was closed, he might complain to his publisher. Then they'd complain to me. Then I'd simply be annoyed for quite a while.

Shooting texts off to everyone seemed impersonal and unprofessional, not to mention confusing. But it was the most efficient method. So, I made a decision and took the unprofessional route, determined I'd made the right choice. Meeting with each person individually would have been a nightmare and taken too much time, so I felt justified in my actions. From the responses I got to my texts, no one seemed to mind my methods.

Rattlesnatches had—wisely—kept his distance from me since attempting to maul me the night before. He had even slept further away at the foot of the bed than usual the night before. However, when I retrieved his harness from the hook by the door and shook it, he appeared suddenly from the depths of the bookstore. Trotting happily over to me, he sat at my feet, waiting to be strapped in for a walk.

Begrudgingly, since it's bad taste to physically fight a cat as revenge for being mauled, I put the harness on my furry companion. Rattlesnatches stretched and preened at my feet once the harness was latched on, as if preparing himself for an Olympic event. I waited patiently for him to complete his stretches, and then opened the door wide. The toasty summer air greeted us as Rattlesnatches pranced out onto the sidewalk. For a moment, I was concerned that maybe the concrete was too hot for his little paws, but when he showed no signs of discomfort, I closed the shop door behind us.

Making sure the door locked behind us, I led us down the sidewalk to Charlene's. Baffled by the incredibly brief amount of walking before we stopped, Rattlesnatches stood beside me at the chocolate shop's door, confused. I pulled open the brown front door of the shop and stepped inside, giving Rattlesnatches' leash a light tug to get him to follow. Still confused by the short trip, Rattlesnatches' tiptoed inside behind me.

Charlene's Chocolates is typically cooler than any other shop on Harbor Street due to the wares being peddled. No one wants half-melted chocolate treats. However, due to the sudden influx of summer weather, the store felt chillier than usual. Though it was midday on a Wednesday, Charlene actually had a customer ducking out of the store as I entered, and another waiting at the counter to be helped. Fortunately, the customer waiting to be helped turned out to be Lila Westbrook, so I knew I wouldn't have to wait to speak to Charlene.

In fact, when Charlene stepped over to help Lila, her eyes caught mine and she spoke.

"Oh!" Charlene exclaimed. "Jackson! Do you need some treats, too? Oh. And…you brought your cat. Lovely."

Doing all I could to not roll my eyes as Lila turned at the mention of my name, I waved Charlene off.

"I didn't want to stay in here long since we're off on a walk," I explained as Lila came over, crouched down, and gave Rattlesnatches scratches. "I was just going to get a dozen truffles once you're done helping Lila."

Lila, looking up from her spot beside Rattlesnatches, smiled at me.

"You go ahead, Jackson," she said. "I have this one to entertain me."

"You sure?" I asked.

She gestured for me to go ahead, so I handed her Rattlesnatches' leash and stepped up to the glass counter in front of me. I didn't really want any chocolates and wasn't particularly hungry, but considering what I was about to do, I felt it best to spend some money in Charlene's shop.

"Could I get a half dozen of your coconut truffles?" I asked her.

"Sure thing," Charlene said. "A dozen is only five dollars more."

Smiling as best I could, I pretended to be awed.

"A dozen it is then!" I announced jubilantly.

Smiling, Charlene set about grabbing a box and stepped over to slide back the door on the case to select a dozen of her coconut truffles. I watched patiently as she used the sanitary tongs to select the treats I would probably give to my mother or someone else.

"Your friend sure is a handful," Lila announced from behind me.

Turning, I found her kneeling on the floor, fawning over Rattlesnatches, not looking at me.

"I'm sorry?" I asked.

"Oh," Lila said, glancing up briefly, "that author person. He's a bit much, isn't he?"

Chuckling, I nodded.

"He seems to be a handful," I agreed. "But he'll only be here until Monday morning. I think."

"Let us pray." Lila shook her head. "He's been bellyaching and moaning since yesterday."

"About what?" I asked, glancing over my shoulder to make sure Charlene was still selecting truffles and not simply waiting on me.

Lila looked up at me, rolled her eyes and stood. She walked over and handed Rattlesnatches' leash to me.

"*The drivers in this town*," Lila said in a mocking tone. "Says he almost got *mowed down* by someone yesterday."

I chuckled.

"You can laugh," Lila said, folding her arms over her chest playfully, "but he called the police and even made a report about it."

It was my turn to roll my eyes. "I'm sure it was nothing."

"Absolutely," Lila said. "He got upset today because he could smell bleach on the towels. They're white. What does he think they get washed with? Of course he can't find *any food* worth eating in this town. And he's *terribly upset* that the *one source of culture* in this town—The Downtown—isn't going to be open for a while yet."

Laughing, I held my hands up defensively.

"If I'd known he'd be so fussy, I wouldn't have bothered," I said. "Or I would have asked someone else to come for a signing."

Lila sighed and forced a smile to her face. "Well, he's paid up full and he's bringing in tourists on Sunday, I'm sure. We'll endure."

I reached out and gave her shoulder a squeeze. She gave me a wink as Charlene cleared her throat, getting my attention. Turning, I dug in my wallet and produced my credit card to pay. Once my payment had gone through and my box of truffles was bagged up, I did what I'd actually come to Charlene's to do.

"Can you keep them at the counter for me?" I asked her. "After our walk, I'll swing back by to grab them. Don't want to take them out in the heat or go home first."

"Sure thing," Charlene said, setting the bag to the side. "I'm here 'til six."

"I'll be back way before then," I said with a chuckle. "Also, I wanted to let you know personally—"

I leaned in and lowered by voice for dramatic effect, then waved Lila over so as to seemingly indoctrinate them into a secret club. Lila sidled up beside me to listen.

"The coffee bar is opening Tuesday when we open for regular hours," I said. "I have a new barista named Angel. He's a genius. You'll want to stop by and try his coffee. It's delicious."

Charlene's and Lila's eyes lit up.

"But don't tell too many people," I said in a hushed tone. "We don't want things to get too crazy on the first day, right?"

Charlene was nodding her head emphatically immediately and Lila followed suit. Smiling at them both, I thanked them for their promise of discretion, then said my goodbyes. Grinning to myself as Rattlesnatches and I made our way back outside, I knew I'd started the Prayer Chain. By Tuesday morning, Charlene would have the town whipped into a frenzy and our first day of coffee sales would be through the roof. Hopefully, Angel would be able to keep up.

With the thought that the first day the coffee bar was opened would be landmark business for Head Rock Harbor Books, I led Rattlesnatches along the sidewalk. The two of us walked—well, one of us pranced, and it wasn't me—until we reached the corner. Turning south, I let Rattlesnatches lead us across the street and down towards Harbor Stage. With my furry companion able to lead us, I mentally checked out.

As Rattlesnatches led us through town, garnering waves and greetings from people we passed, I was making a list in my head of chores I needed to accomplish. By the time Taylor C. Tomlin was signing books in the shop on Sunday night, I wanted to be prepared for the week following Pride. I wanted the store dusted, swept, floors shined, and organized beautifully for a fresh week. My apartment and bathroom needed to be sparkling clean. And if I was going to have a busy week with a new coffee bar, and hopefully lots of books sold, my fridge would need to be stocked.

We'd made our way to Harper's by the time Rattlesnatches had decided he'd walked through town enough. I was starting a list in my head of what I needed to pick up at the grocery store when my guide turned us back towards the north end of town. Following along behind him, I took out my phone and began tapping out an actual grocery list was we walked. Though I trusted my mind quite a bit, it was always best to make a list when going to the grocery store. Otherwise, I ended up bringing home the entirety of aisle twelve. Which happened to be where all the unhealthy snacks were stocked.

By the time we'd gotten back to Harbor Stage, I'd finished my list and slipped my phone back into my pocket. Rattlesnatches was still prancing, but he'd slowed his gait. Approaching the walkway up to Harbor Stage, Rattlesnatches stopped in the street along the curb and began sniffing at a small pile of detritus along the cement buffer. I paused, letting him sate his curiosity. The grocery shopping wasn't so urgent that I couldn't let Rattlesnatches play around a bit.

However, once he'd finished sniffing around, then sat back on his haunches and turned his head up to look at me, I also became curious. Rattlesnatches gave me a slow blink of his amber eyes, then meowed softly up at me. Frowning, I knelt down next to the pile of old leaves and grass in the gutter. Rattlesnatches looked down at the pile, as if asking me to inspect it.

"Good grief," I mumbled. "What did you find now that has you so interested?"

Brushing my fingers gently through the pile, careful in case there was anything sharp, I felt the tips of my fingers run over something that felt like smooth metal. My brow raised with interest, I dug into the pile and my fingers wrapped around an object too heavy to be yard leavings. When I pulled my hand out of the pile, a shiny silver object sparkled between my fingers.

A lug nut.

Laughing, I pinched the object between my fingers and held it out to Rattlesnatches. He leaned forward to sniff it, then looked up at me and meowed once more.

"That's what got your interest?" I shook my head and stood. "A lug nut?"

He stared up at me.

"Wait until you hear about cars," I said, slipping the metal object into my hip pocket. "It'll blow your mind."

Rattlesnatches stood from his seated position and turned towards Harbor Street again. However, before he took off, he turned his head to stare at Harbor Stage intently. I twisted my head to look up the walk towards the building and found Randall and Michael on the porch. I lifted my hand and waved, and they returned the gesture. When Rattlesnatches still made no effort to move, I walked ahead, tugging gently at the leash. He got the point and trotted after me, picking up his pace until he was in the lead, prancing once again.

Within two minutes, we were picking up the unwanted, yet paid for, truffles from Charlene. As she made promises once again to keep the coffee bar secret under her hat, I thanked her and exited her shop. Grinning from her shop to the bookstore, I knew her insisting that she would keep things quiet meant exactly the opposite. By the time I let us into the bookstore, set the truffles on the check-out counter, and pulled the harness from Rattlesnatches, he was in a frenzy.

Dashing up the stairs to the apartment as soon as he was free, I knew that he was headed for his water bowl and the foot of my bed for a nap. I hung the harness and leash back on the hook by the front door and locked it. Then I pulled the lug nut from my pocket and set it on the counter next to the box of truffles. Patting my pockets, I found that I still had my wallet and my keys, so I headed through the dark shop towards the backdoor.

While Rattlesnatches slept, I would head off to the grocery store and complete one of my chores before midday arrived. Armed with the list on my phone, I knew I could get the groceries purchased, come home, put them away, and then make a healthy homemade meal for lunch. Saving money, and probably calories, I'd stay away from Munchies Café and Harper's for at least one day. I zipped through the backdoor and locked it behind me.

As I turned to the red Beetle, I found it impossible to open the driver's door. Not because anything was wrong with the car or my keys, but because of the man slumped on the ground against it.

Though I didn't do anything to confirm the fact, I could tell the man slumped against my car was dead.

The knife sticking out of his chest made that fact evident.

Checking his pulse seemed unnecessary.

Chapter Ten

Marv was in a snit once more. For the second day in a row, I was treated to his frenzied pacing. Jeremy and Ashley were surveying the scene in the alley behind the bookstore. I was sitting on the stoop right outside the backdoor of the shop, and Deacon, having barely arrived, was gloving up. Marv was marching up and down the alley, muttering incoherently to himself as the rest of us remained silent. Since there was a very dead man laid against the side of my car. Silence seemed to be the respectable thing.

Officer Ashley Riley seemed focused on the scene, taking in the details, and making sure he was immersed in his work. Jeremy spent his time between looking over the scene and shooting me looks out of the corner of his eye. Deacon, as was usual for him when he was on scene, was all business. Though he had greeted me with a nod of his head and a smile, he had gotten straight to work, as one would expect of a professional forensics technician. Marv, on the other hand, had done nothing to hide his frustration with the predicament in which we'd found ourselves.

As far as I knew, Rattlesnatches was up in the apartment, snoozing happily at the foot of my bed, his belly full of water and kibbles. I hadn't gone back inside since I'd stepped out the backdoor to head to the grocery store. As soon as my eyes landed on the dead man beside my car, I pulled my phone from my pocket and made a discreet call to Jeremy. Though it wasn't exactly protocol to call a detective directly when one finds a dead body, I knew that going through dispatch and talking to Gloria would only make matters worse. By the time I'd hung up the phone, she would have started spreading the gossip.

Making the decision to inform Jeremy discretely and directly of the situation, I felt that points would be earned. Maybe Marv would be less irritated with me, and Jeremy would feel more empathy for my situation. However, from what I could tell, me simply finding a dead body was enough to put me firmly on both of their lists. Though I could tell they didn't suspect me of having anything to do with the reason the man was dead and slumped against my car, I may as well have been the suspect. Ashley seemed indifferent to his coworkers, and empathetic to my situation.

"Hurry up, hurry up!" Marv grumbled as he paced. *"We need to get the meat wagon in here and get this guy out of here before anyone else sees him."*

I shook my head but said nothing.

"Just got here, Chief," Deacon said, keeping his tone even.

Marv growled with frustration but didn't bark back anything else. Deacon shot me a look, rolled his eyes, then knelt down next to the body. I gave him a sympathetic smile before looking down at my feet. I pulled my knees up to my chest and wrapped my arms around them as I sat on the stoop and kept my eyes anywhere but on the man against my car.

Though I hadn't meant to, I'd seen plenty before Jeremy had come roaring up to the alley behind Harbor Street, parking the cruiser so it blocked the entrance. I'd had nothing to do but sit there and stare at him for a solid three minutes, after all. I was no detective or forensics tech, but I had a pretty good eye and a solid memory. Everything that could be noticed, I'd noticed. All of it was committed to memory.

College-aged young man, black swath of hair, maybe six feet tall, slim build, tan skin, eyes rheumy from death, orange swim suit, white tank top, cowrie shell bracelet. One of his brown leather flip flops had held on, but the other's strap had snapped and had fallen from his foot. The knife was anything you'd find in anyone's kitchen. Brown wooden handle, the part of the blade showing looked to be a typical butcher's blade. There was enough blood pooled around the man that it was obvious he'd been killed next to my car, and the hit had been solid.

Straight into the heart.

He'd probably had seconds before he bled out and died. Though it couldn't have felt great, getting stabbed in the chest and left to die, he probably hadn't suffered long.

I desperately wanted to tell someone to close his eyes. But I knew that asking them to do anything with the body before all the apparent evidence was collected would upset Marv. Having him even angrier with me would only make my life harder. I was trying to avoid such things lately. If someone hadn't killed a man behind my shop, I would have been crushing it.

"Does this one have a wallet on him?" Jeremy asked.

I looked up at the sound of my friend's voice.

Deacon glanced up at Jeremy, then reached under the man. Digging around for a moment, he grunted slightly.

"No pockets in the back. No wallet," Deacon said as he felt along the outer thighs of the man's swimsuit. "No hip pockets."

"I don't see anywhere else he'd be hiding his I.D.," Ashley said.

"Well, if he's one of the tourists here for Pride, maybe it's in an orifice," Marv grumbled. "I'm sure I don't have to say which one."

All four of us turned our heads, shooting him a look of disgust.

Marv rolled his eyes and went back to pacing. Jeremy, Deacon, and I all exchanged concerned looks as Ashley went back to examining the victim and the scene. Annoyed with the entire situation—and sad for the man—I slowly rose from the stoop. Jeremy's eyes were on me immediately.

"What are you doing?" he asked.

"Going inside?" I shrugged. "Do you need me for anything else?"

"You haven't even given a statement," Jeremy said.

"Oh, let him go," Marv grumbled, pacing and waving his hands erratically. "He didn't do this."

I gestured vaguely at Marv, trying to hide my irritation.

"There ya' go," I said. "I didn't do this. Even Marv knows it. What else could you possibly need from me?"

"A witness statement," Jeremy said evenly, flashing eyes at Marv. "I need to get a statement from you."

"For crying out loud, Morris," Marv barked. "Leave it be! Let's tag it and bag it!"

Jeremy, suddenly crimson cheeked, looked down at the notepad in his hand, his pen poised over the page. I shrugged again, mostly to myself. Before I could turn and open the backdoor to the shop, Marv marched over, his face nearly the same shade as Jeremy's, and jabbed a finger at me.

"You keep this to yourself, Jackson," he demanded. "You hear me? We don't need anything getting out about this."

I stared blankly at him.

"You don't tell Charlene, my daughter, Shirley, Lardell, Henry, nobody on this street! Don't even say a word to that damn cat of yours!" Marv growled his orders at me as if I was on his payroll.

"Marv," I said calmly, though my mind was reeling with a plethora of devastating quips, "I called Jeremy instead of Gloria so this *wouldn't* get spread around town. You're barking at the wrong dog right now."

He glared at me for a moment, and though he tried to hide it, I saw his expression soften for the briefest of moments. No matter what our mayor had been whispering in his ear about me, the real, logical Marv was still in there somewhere. He knew that I wasn't going to be a problem, though he had plenty.

Marv started to open his mouth, shut it, then jabbed his finger at me again. Apparently, he felt that finished making his point, because he marched away to begin pacing once again.

"Can I use your bathroom, Jackson?" Ashley asked.

"Help yourself," I said, tapping the code into the keypad by the door and then stepping aside so he could slip by me through the backdoor.

"Jackson?" I sighed at the sound of my name coming from Deacon.

I turned and looked at him.

"Yeah?" I asked.

"You still making dinner for us tonight?" Deacon asked.

Jeremy's head immediately rose and his eyes shot to me. I was about to give Deacon a confused look, but something in his eyes warned me. Instead of giving him the quizzical look, asking any questions, or looking at Jeremy, I simply nodded.

"Seven o'clock," I nodded. "Just as we planned. As long as…you know…you're done here and everything."

Deacon gave me a tight smile, nodded, and went back to his work. Jeremy, still with flaming cheeks, squinted down at Deacon. When I saw his head turning, intending to give me a similar look, I turned before he could look into my eyes and see any semblance of deceit there. I tapped in the backdoor code once more, grabbed the handle, and pulled the backdoor open.

"Leave it unlocked," Jeremy requested from behind me. "In case we need to pop our head in and holler for you again."

"You all know the code," I grumbled. "It doesn't matter."

Stepping inside, I ignored him, but I didn't lock the door so code access was deactivated. I pulled the door shut quickly behind me, slamming it as hard as I could, hoping that everyone outside would hear my anger in the action. Making it clear that I was inside my business and wanted to be left alone was my intention, and I hoped it was clear. As I was fuming by the door, Ashley came rushing by, grinning sheepishly as he excused himself around me and out the backdoor.

As I made my way into the shop, my mind was reeling and my stomach was rolling. The image of the man slumped against my car, the knife sticking out of his chest, was burned into the back of my eyes. I could still smell the metallic, iron-y smell of blood. And other things that the body expels after death.

Aside from the obvious trauma of finding yet another dead body—another gruesome one at that—Deacon had thrown me for a loop. The look he'd given me when he'd asked if we were still on for an imaginary date had my mind reeling. Why had he pretended we had a dinner date planned in front of the other guys? Especially Jeremy? And what had the look meant that he shot me when I went to respond?

I felt I was going insane.

Cozy mysteries, crime thrillers, and detective stories were some of my favorites—in all their forms. T.V. shows, movies, podcasts, and especially books, that fell within the genre were what really got my blood pumping. There could never be enough for me to consume. Give me Jessica Fletcher and the quaint little coastal town of Cabot Cove, some pizza, a six pack of sugary soda, and a comfy seat, and I could escape the world for hours.

Slipping between the pages with Arly Hanks or Claire Malloy or Miss Marple or Hercule Poirot had costs me days off of my life. Time well spent, as far as I was concerned. Tuning into *Unsolved Mysteries*, *Forensic Files*, or *The First*

48 could pass an entire evening for me. I'd lost weekends of my life to such shows.

My free time in college wasn't spent at ragers, frat parties, or bonfires. I'd spent my time in my twin bed in my dorm, laptop next to me, eating chips, and watching crime shows. Or I'd curled up under the covers with a novel. It was what had inspired me to start writing the first Detective Randy Melton book in my junior year. I'd spent endless hours, days, weeks, months—maybe even an entire year of my life dedicated to consuming crime fiction and non-fiction.

But there was one thing that media never discussed—but especially the cozies. Amateur sleuths in those shows and books never suffer trauma. No one ever talks about what finding dead bodies and dealing with the violence humans are capable of inflicting on each other can do to the mind. Walking through the bookstore, I felt nauseated. I felt angry. I felt sad. I felt annoyed.

I felt everything.

And there was no one to talk to about it.

Going to Jeremy and unloading my feelings about all of the recent death in our little town would do me no good. Cops are bred to ignore those feelings—at least openly. If they talk to a counselor about their feelings, they keep that to themselves. Cops don't have feelings. Feelings get you put on paid administrative leave. Possibly indefinitely.

Reaching up to run my fingers through my curls, I couldn't help but laugh at my next thought. Obviously, groceries were going to have to wait. Whatever Deacon expected me to make for our impromptu dinner date, I hoped he wasn't expecting anything fancy. Sighing as I let my hand run over and over through my dark brown curls, as though soothing myself, I made my way to the stairs. However, as I laid a hand on the post to turn and go up the stairs, a thump behind me stopped me dead in my tracks.

Spinning anxiously, my eyes darted around the dim bookstore. The late morning sun through the windows provided just enough light for me to see around the store clearly enough, but it was dark enough that it took a moment for me to find the source of the noise. A light blue book was on the floor at the end of the Young Adult section.

Walking over, I knelt down and snatched the book up off of the ground. *The Fault in Our Stars* by John Green. I held the book in my hand as I turned my head to look up at the bookcase. Rattlesnatches was sitting on his haunches at the top of the shelf, staring down at me. I glared up at him and stuffed the book back into the slot from which he'd knocked it out.

"Look here you little demon." I hissed up at him. "I don't need any nonsense from you for the rest of the day. You hear me?"

His amber eyes stared down at me, boredom plastered across his triangular face. However, I could tell he had gotten the message.

"Good," I said.

Then I did my best Marv impersonation and marched to the stairs, straight up them, and into the apartment.

Chapter Eleven

Dinners on warm summer nights are best when you have to turn on the stove or oven as little as possible. It's a pretty easy task to accomplish if you have been to the grocery store and have prepared for meals that don't require much heat to make. Since a dead man had kept me from getting to the grocery store as planned, I had to get creative. I wasn't blaming the dead man for the predicament I'd found myself in presently. He probably didn't want to be dead. However, Deacon inviting himself to dinner *after finding the dead man* had put me in a spot.

Since I had to throw together a dinner at the last minute, what I already had in my fridge and cabinets would have to do. I'd taken a long nap upon coming inside after being chased out of the alley by Marv. Once I'd woken up, gotten a shower and dressed in fresh clothes, I assessed the ingredients I had at my disposal. Some fresh veggies, pasta, and enough ingredients to make a decent vinaigrette meant that a summer pasta salad would be dinner. Having recently purchased a baguette from Henry Mathis at Pain, I decided I would slice it up, toast it, and serve it on the side with some herb butter.

I wasn't certain how particular Deacon was with food, but since he had been the one to put me on the spot, that wasn't my problem. If the dinner I threw together wasn't to his liking, he knew where all the local restaurants and fast-food joints were located. He could always stop by the Casey's for pizza after he left my place if he wanted.

So, I set about making the pasta and slicing up the baguette an hour before he was set to arrive. Unfortunately, Jeremy had insisted on coming by for my witness statement around the same time. Informing him that he would have to question me while I cooked, he drove over from the police department to talk to me.

"Is that all you remember?" Jeremy asked as he continued to lean against the doorjamb.

He was writing in his notepad as I poured the dry pasta into the pot of boiling water.

"You just walked outside and there he was?" Jeremy said, as if unsure I hadn't forgotten something.

"That's it," I said through clenched teeth, staring down at the pot of water. "I walked out the backdoor, locked it, and then saw him. It was maybe thirty seconds before I called you."

"Why thirty seconds?" Jeremy asked.

"It took that long to process what I was seeing," I sighed, closing my eyes in frustration. "At first, I thought he could be a drunk tourist. Then I saw the hilt of the knife and realized he wasn't drunk. Or, if he was, that wasn't why he was laying against my car."

Jeremy continued to write.

"And while I waited for you, I sat there on the steps and stared at him," I said. "I didn't touch him, the car, or anything else except the steps and the backdoor."

My best friend nodded along as I spoke.

"Any idea why someone would be behind your shop, getting murdered?" Jeremy looked up, an eyebrow raised.

I turned my head to stare at him blankly, my left hand still stirring the pot of pasta.

"Okay," Jeremy said.

"I don't even know who he is," I said. "He...I don't know."

My phone dinged. I slipped it from my pocket to find a text from Deacon.

On my way!

I tapped out a response.

Front door is unlocked. Let yourself in. I'll be upstairs cooking.

Jeremy eyed me for a moment as I locked my phone and slid it back into my hip pocket. I thought about what I was about to say and swallowed it down, something inside of me telling me to keep that particular thought to myself. Instead of saying anything else—even if it might help the investigation—I turned my attention back to the pot of water and pasta. I could feel Jeremy's cop stare boring into the side of my head as I did my best to ignore him.

"You were about to say something there," Jeremy said. "What was it?"

"I don't know who he is," I said. "Was. I don't know him."

"But…you suspect something," Jeremy said, pushing away from the doorjamb and stepping further into the apartment.

"Jeremy," I said with a sigh, turning to him, "stop."

"What?" he asked.

His eyes went wide and shiny and his bottom lip jutted out ever so. I'd known my friend since we were children. His puppy-dog expression could work on women, the men he wanted to sleep with, and other witnesses. It didn't work on me.

"I told you everything I know," I said. "And it's been made clear to me that my involvement—*in any way*—with these murders is unwelcome. Even you made it clear at the PD yesterday that I needed to back off. So…*let me back off.*"

With a sigh, Jeremy lowered his pen and notepad, his arms dangling at his sides. It took him a moment to lose the puppy dog expression, but it finally melted from his face. He stared at me a moment longer as he robotically returned his pen and notepad to his pocket.

I turned back to the pot of boiling pasta on the stove.

"Jacks—"

"No, Jeremy," I said firmly, keeping my eyes on the water. "I've given you my witness statement. I told you everything I know. Unless you've surmised from that information that I'm somehow guilty of committing a crime, I'm done with this."

The barely suppressed rage coming off of my best friend seemed to fill the room. Or it could have been the steam wafting up into my face from the boiling pot of pasta. Either way, I could see Jeremy in the corner of my eye, considering his choices. I knew one of those choices wasn't whether or not to arrest me. No matter how angry I made him, he knew with certainty that I hadn't committed any crimes, let alone murder.

However, I could tell he was fighting a battle in his head over whether to keep pressing me for my thoughts or to let the entire conversation drop. Fortunately, Jeremy was smart enough to know that he and his boss had painted themselves into a corner. I'd been labeled a problem that needed to be handled. They'd made it clear that my help with their cases was no longer welcome.

Pressing me to talk about the murder beyond my witness statement would require admitting that they had been wrong. Jeremy wasn't going to do that. Even without Marv present to witness it and threaten his badge over it, Jeremy wasn't going to risk the trouble he'd get into by saying such a thing. For the time being, he was going to have to go along with the mess Marv had gotten them both into by listening to whatever it was our mayor had been whispering in his ear.

What has she been saying to Marv? I found myself wondering.

Mayor Linda Wagner had gone out of her way to practically force me into organizing the first annual Pride Weekend for Head Rock Harbor. I'd done as she desired. Now that there were more murders in town, she was making me a pariah to the police department. I simply couldn't wrap my head around it.

"Well," Jeremy said, barely controlling his voice, "if you think of anything else, you'll contact me?"

"Of course," I said.

I didn't look over at him. My eyes stayed on the pasta.

"You know the way out," I said. "I've got to finish cooking."

Jeremy stood there for a few moments, staring at me, as I watched him out of the corner of my eye. Finally, he threw his hands up, sighed, and stomped out of the apartment. Closing my eyes and shaking my head, I tried to slough the frustration away. If Jeremy was going to be upset with me, he only had himself to blame. And Marv. I was only doing what they had made clear they wanted me to do.

His feet thudded pointedly on each step down into the shop, across the shop itself, and then I heard the bell ding over the door. I was too far away to make it out, but he said something as he was exiting the shop, and I heard the bell jangle once more. Lifting the pot from the stove, I took it over to the sink to the waiting colander. As I was pouring the contents into the colander, and doing my best to avoid a steam facial, lighter, jauntier footsteps sounded on the stairs.

Turning to look towards the door as the last of the pot's contents slipped into the colander, I saw a smiling Deacon step up to the open doorway. Smiling back at him, I set the pot on the counter and waved him inside.

"Come on in," I said.

Deacon bounded into the room happily. Unlike Jeremy's sad little puppy dog, Deacon's energy was that of a puppy dog happy to be seen. I couldn't help but grin as he made his way across the apartment and slid into a seat at the kitchen table.

"Whatcha cookin', good lookin'?" he asked.

Rolling my eyes with mirth, I lifted the colander to help the pasta drain.

"Well, due to my poor timing, a warm pasta salad," I said. "I'd hoped to make it and get it chilled a bit before you arrived, but…"

I trailed off.

"I saw the *but* on my way in," Deacon snorted. "He nearly ran me down coming out of the shop."

I sighed and dumped the contents of the colander into the large bowl that contained the veggies and dressing I'd already mixed together.

"Let's just say he wasn't happy I didn't have much to give him about the guy in the alley," I said.

"Well," Deacon asked, "what is it he thought you knew? You found a body and immediately called him. What else can you say?"

I shrugged.

But in the back of my mind, I was thinking the one thing I had refused to tell Jeremy. The dead guy slumped against my car had startled me not simply because he had a knife sticking out of his chest. I wasn't simply startled at finding another dead body, either. The thing that had bothered me the most upon stumbling upon the body was that I had thought…for the briefest of moments…that it was Taylor C. Tomlin dead against my car.

The dead man and Taylor resembled each other greatly.

"I don't know," I said, shaking my head clear of thoughts. "But I said what I knew. And that's all there is to it."

Deacon watched me as I stirred the pasta with the sauce and veggies, then put the bowl on the table I'd set before his arrival. Back over at the stove, I opened the oven and pulled out the now toasted slices of baguette. I made sure that the stovetop and oven were both off, then went over to the counter to slide the toasted bread slices in a cloth-lined basket.

When I turned back to the table and sank into the chair, I set the basket of bread next to the bowl of pasta and gave Deacon my full attention. I'd set out plates, silverware, glasses of water, and napkins. The dead man behind the shop had kept me from having any beer or wine on hand, so I hoped that Deacon didn't want to drink with dinner.

"Well," I said, "it is what it is. Dig in."

Deacon chuckled.

"I kind of put you on the spot," he agreed, reaching for the serving spoon sticking out of the pasta bowl. "Sorry about that."

Watching Deacon serve himself a pile of the veggie pasta salad, along with several of the toasted baguette slices, I was struck by the amount of food he planned to consume. He wasn't as scrawny as I, but he was shorter. Seeing if he managed to put away all of the food he'd served himself was going to be fun, in a twisted kind of way. However, Deacon had been working all day, and I wasn't sure when he'd last gotten to eat. Maybe he was simply starving.

"Why did you?" I asked, taking the serving spoon from him once he was done. "Put me on the spot, I mean? Why the imaginary dinner date?"

Serving myself a fairly respectable portion of pasta and a few slices of bread, I waited as Deacon shoveled several forkfuls of pasta into his mouth. Chewing rapidly, he was trying to get as much food into his belly to satisfy his hunger before answering my question. He wasn't avoiding what I'd asked him, so I tried to be patient. He was simply too hungry to ignore the food for longer than was absolutely necessary.

After several mouthfuls of pasta made their way to his gut, Deacon took a gulp of his water and sat back, a slice of bread in his hand. I pointed at the small dish of herb butter I'd laid on the table and Deacon's eyes lit up. He grabbed his butter knife from the side of his plate and plowed a line through the butter.

"Thanks," he said hungrily, smearing the butter on the bread. "It'll be even tastier with butter."

He took a quick bite of the buttered bread and smiled over at me as he chewed. I couldn't help but chuckle, however, my patience had hit its limit.

"So?" I asked. "What's up with the imaginary dinner date?"

Deacon chewed hastily and swallowed, then a sigh escaped his throat.

"Not that I didn't want to spend an evening with you," Deacon began, "but I wanted to talk to you about something."

"I'll try to not get too in my own feelings," I teased as I brought my fork to my mouth.

As I slid the pasta into my mouth, Deacon laughed.

"Look," he said, "I kind of noticed the tension between you, Jeremy, and Marv."

I produced wide, shocked eyes. Deacon chuckled again.

"Yeah," he said, "I know. I must be crazy observant."

"Shocked that anyone would have even noticed," I stated blandly.

"Well," Deacon said, ignoring my sarcasm, "I felt, I don't know, compelled to tell you something. I wasn't going to before, but after today...well, I think you ought to know."

I raised my brow, indicating he should continue as I dug my fork into my pasta.

"Marv doesn't know I know this," Deacon said. "I don't think Jeremy or Ashley know, either."

"Know what?" I urged him on. "Stop beating around the bush."

Another chuckle from Deacon, but he soldiered on.

"Linda," Deacon said, leveling me with his eyes. "The mayor."

"Yeah?"

"A couple weeks ago," Deacon began, nibbling at his bread, "I had stopped by the department to drop off some reports and pick up some evidence. Linda Wagner was in Marv's office, chewing him a new one."

"What about?" I asked, more curious than I told myself hours ago I was allowed to be.

"She got a call from some reporter up in Dubuque, right?" Deacon explained. "I guess she knew someone who lived here and they mentioned Prescott Pemberton and his assistant, uh—"

"Marshelle Martin," I said, remembering the dead man's dead assistant vividly.

When you find the body of a woman lying in a creek, dead, after her employer was murdered, everything about them tends to get branded in your memories.

"Right." Deacon nodded. "Well, I guess they were questioning her about it because the person who tipped off the reporter told them that the police had to have *you* solve the cases."

Immediately, I laid my fork on my plate, and my head rolled back on my shoulders so that was I was staring up at the ceiling. An annoyed groan escaped my throat. Deacon took the interruption as an opportunity to shovel more bread and pasta into his mouth. Once my groan tapered off, I brought my eyes back to Deacon.

"And Linda suspects that I'm the one who tipped off the reporter?" I asked, shaking my head.

"Possibly?" Deacon shrugged as he spoke around a mouthful of pasta. "Or that you told someone who told someone who—"

"No wonder," I said, picking up my fork once more.

Deacon nodded along sympathetically.

"Regardless," Deacon said, "if I were you, the next time you find a body...no you didn't. Sneak away and let someone else report it."

I couldn't help but chuckle evilly at the suggestion.

"Hard to do when the body is propped against your car," I said bitterly.

"True," Deacon said. "But you catch my drift. Keep your head down. Once Pride Weekend is over, I don't think Linda will have much use else for you. She's convinced herself that you're a problem and that's all there is to it. And she's going to do everything she can to convince everyone at the police department of the same thing now that you've organized Pride for her."

"Well," I said, "I guess she got what she wanted out of me."

Deacon made a sad, agreeable sound, but there was nothing else he could really say that would be comforting. Due to one reporter calling about the sudden uptick of deaths in Head Rock Harbor, the mayor had convinced herself— and Marv—that I was going around bad mouthing them to the news. Though I couldn't think of a single reason why they would assume I was behind the reporter's tip. What purpose would I have in tipping off a reporter?

What goal or reward would be in it for me?

For several moments, Deacon and I ate in silence. I wasn't sure if Deacon was on the same train of thought as me, but he was clever. If I knew what he knew, he'd probably followed the same train of thought that I had. He was also wondering why Linda had zeroed in on me as the person who had contacted the reporter. Obviously, there was no clear reason why I would do such a thing. Free marketing for the bookstore, possibly?

If that had been the case, why hadn't I seen an uptick in customers from out of town?

Linda's logic was skewed. Marv believing her theory was ridiculous. However, I knew both of them well enough to know that they were like a squirrel with a nut. They were not going to let go of the theory that I was a problem until solid evidence was smashed into their faces.

"Well," I said, admitting defeat, "I didn't even want to organize Pride to begin with. If this is what it takes to make Marv and Linda act like I don't exist after next weekend, so be it. I don't care if they think I'm talking to reporters."

Deacon smiled softly at me.

"You don't not care."

"Well, no," I admitted. "But it's all I've got right now."

My dinner companion stared at me for a few moments, then an evil grin overtook his face.

"You ever hear the story about the bird who waited too long to fly south for winter?" he suddenly asked.

"Uh...no?" I grinned cautiously.

By the time Deacon was getting up to leave an hour later, I was still laughing at his story. We said "goodbye" numerous times as he left the apartment, giving each other a warm hug at the door. Then I watched from the balcony as he made his way down into the dark shop and the door that led out into the dark night.

"Oh!" I shouted down at him as he stood in the rectangle of light the apartment door cast into the shop below. "Hey!"

Deacon stopped and turned to smile up at me, his teeth showing brilliantly in the golden glow from the apartment.

"Yeah?" he asked, too optimistically.

I ignored his eagerness.

"There's a box of coconut truffles from Charlene's on the counter there," I said. "Next to a lug nut. They're yours. For cheering me up."

Deacon smiled and stepped out of the rectangle of light to the counter. I watched him in the shadows, retrieving the box from the check-out counter. When he stepped back into the light, he held it aloft with a grateful salute.

"I didn't see a lug nut," Deacon chuckled, "but I never turn down candy. Even if it's not as good as a cup of coffee."

I gave him a warning smile, but it held no actual anger. Deacon chuckled evilly, saluted with the box again, then made his way out of the shop. Suddenly frowning once Deacon's statement registered in my head, I found myself walking down the stairs to the store below. I went over to the door and slapped on the lights.

Over at the check-out counter, I looked all over the top of it and around both sides. Deacon hadn't seen a lug nut because it had disappeared. Perplexed, and a bit concerned, I went over to the front door and locked it. Then I went to the backdoor and locked it tightly, jiggling the handle to make sure it was secure. Back in the shop, I shut off the lights and dashed back up the stairs to the apartment. When I got back to the door into my apartment, I found Rattlesnatches sitting on his haunches, staring up at me, yawning.

Laughing quietly, I let him lead me into the apartment. For the first time in months, I closed the apartment door and locked it. I'd sleep better knowing there were as many barriers between me and the outside world as possible.

Chapter Twelve

My first chore of the day on Thursday was a trip to the Hy-Vee for the groceries I hadn't gotten the day before. Fortunately, when I went out to the Beetle, I didn't find another dead body. Even more fortuitously, neither Jeremy nor Marv had taken my car in as evidence in the man's death. Having Marv and Linda wanting to keep the two recent deaths quiet had behooved me, though I wasn't certain I was entirely happy about it. Regardless, I went to the grocery store and returned an hour later with my reusable grocery bags overflowing with essentials.

By the time I'd put the groceries away, it was mid-morning and my stomach was angry with me. Against Rattlesnatches' protests, I left the shop and went down to Munchies for a platter full of eggs, bacon, toast, and hashbrowns. Once again, the café was full of out-of-towners, along with frustrated and annoyed locals. Taylor C. Tomlin was seated in the center of Munchies with a few other out-of-towners, loudly regaling anyone who would listen with the story of the "sporty black car" that nearly mowed him down in the middle of the street. I kept my head low, hoping he wouldn't notice me.

Due to the looks I was getting from the locals, I ate quickly, tipped greatly, and paid. Shirley didn't treat me any differently, but I knew even she was beginning to tire of Pride Weekend—and it hadn't even begun. Eventually, I knew that she and Lardell would have enough of the hipsters and their questions and unique behaviors. I didn't want to be present when it happened. If Bernie had kicked people out of his bar early in the week, it wouldn't be long before other business owners started to follow suit. Hopefully, we could get through Sunday before too many people got completely fed up with the out-of-towners.

Swarms of young queer people were buzzing around Harbor Street as I made my way back to the shop from Munchies. I had to explain to a handful of them who were window shopping at the bookstore that we wouldn't be open until Sunday night for the book signing with Taylor C. Tomlin. Though they were disappointed, the group didn't press the issue. Assuring me they would all be back Sunday since they had tickets to the signing, I did my best to be friendly. They stuck around to "ooh" and "aah" at Rattlesnatches as he laid in his basket in the front window for a bit.

Once they were gone, I made my way back out of the shop and made my first stop of the day. At Charlene's Chocolates, I checked in to make sure she was ready for Pride Weekend. She mostly wanted to gossip about the coffee bar and the out-of-towners, so I made my exit as quickly as possible. Henry Mathis at Pain was simply excited about all the sales he'd made over the last few days and those he anticipated over the weekend. Pleased to see that not everyone was annoyed with the influx of business, I thanked him and told him to let me know if he needed anything.

Ainsley Bucksworth was polite but cool to me when I stopped in at The Loft. I wasn't certain if it was because her father—Marv—had said anything about me, or if she didn't see the point of getting excited about the out-of-towners. The odds of her upscale home goods store selling much to the tourists were low, so that could also have been the reason for her demeanor. Regardless, I thanked her, told her to let me know if she needed anything, then made my way to my next stop.

Lila Westbrook over at the Inn told me that things were essentially the same as they'd been, though they were struggling to keep up with the demand for fresh towels and other housekeeping duties. However, I could see the dollar signs bouncing in her eyes as she grumbled her frustrations, so I didn't worry too much about her. I gave her the same speech as everyone else and checked in on Michael and Randall Cummings at Harbor Stage. Though they wouldn't be open for Pride, I wanted to make sure that they were prepared for the festivities.

Finding them to be out, a sign on the door proclaiming that they'd be back on Friday if anyone needed them, I moved onto the next business. The folks at The Dock were excited for the food and wine pairings on Saturday evening. Every single seat was sold, earning them a cool mint by even their busiest Saturday standards. Bernie didn't quite chase me out of his tavern, but he made it clear he was trying to keep the out-of-towners out of his place. He was trying to make a safe-space for the locals during Pride Weekend.

I couldn't say that I blamed him.

Lastly, I stopped by the city workers' offices to talk to the maintenance and sanitation workers. They assured me that they were going to be hanging the lights on Harbor Street first thing the following morning. Everything would be in place by the time dark fell on Friday evening.

By the time noon came, I'd walked all over town, talked to every business owner downtown, and my feet were absolutely screaming for a rest. Fortunately, my last stop of the day was at Harper's. Checking in with the owner—my mother—and having lunch would complete my morning chores. Of course, no one had asked me to check in with everyone the day before Pride Weekend, but I felt, as the organizer, it was simply an unspoken, obvious task of mine.

When I entered Harper's, I found out that most of the tourists hadn't quite made their way in for lunch yet. A few tables were taken by locals, who shot me warm grins for once, and a couple of folks were sitting on stools at the bar on the right side of the building. Heidi, the hostess for the restaurant on the left side was nowhere in sight. So, I waved a hand at Cleo St. Clair, the bartender, and she indicated I should take a seat.

"*I'll tell Deb you're here!*" she hollered as she poured a beer into a pint glass from a tap.

I gave her a smile and a nod and headed to my favorite corner booth. I slid across the red vinyl with an exhausted exhale, my feet immediately thankful. Automatically, I grabbed a menu from the holder at the end of the table, though I knew exactly what I was going to get. If it wouldn't have been completely rude, I would have leaned back and kicked my feet up on the booth seat across from me.

However, my mother would have popped me in the back of the head when she arrived, so I avoided getting too comfortable.

When my phone dinged in my pocket, I slid it out and swiped my thumb across the screen. Deacon had texted. Smiling to myself, I opened the text to see what he'd had to say.

If you didn't get enough time with me last night, I'm free tonight, too. I don't want you to get sad if you have to go too long without my company.

I gave an amused snort and tapped out a response.

While I will suffer greatly not seeing you tonight, we'll have to wait to hang out as planned tomorrow evening. I have things I need to finish up at the shop tonight.

His response was immediate.

Bummer. But I get it. I'll pick you up at the shop Friday at 5:30!

I gave him a thumb's up emoji and locked my phone, sliding it back into my hip pocket. As I was putting away my phone, a pair of hands came to rest on the end of the table. Looking up, expecting to see Deb—my mother—I was surprised to see Linda Wagner squinting down at me suspiciously.

"Mayor," I said simply, folding my hands atop the table.

"Jackson," she replied as coolly. "Imagine meeting you here."

"At my mom's bar and grill? Where I get free meals?" I stared up at her. "Inconceivable."

Linda rolled her eyes. Leaning down, she stared directly into my eyes.

"That incident behind your shop?" she said cryptically in case anyone unaware of the dead body I'd found behind my shop was listening. "That falls under the umbrella of things we talked about at the police department."

"Just so we're clear," I said.

She nodded.

"And so we're clear—again—I don't work for the city. Or the police," I said. "I don't take orders from you or Marv."

Linda started to open her mouth.

"However," I said, stopping her, "I have no reason to go around spreading gossip that will make you, the police, or the town look bad. So drop it. Stop bothering me."

"Listen here," Linda's fingers clutched at the side of the table. "I'm warning you Jackson. You keep any thoughts, suspicions, and theories to yourself. Don't go talking to *anyone* about either of the incidents."

I rolled my eyes.

"The City Council gives—*and revokes*—business licenses for Head Rock Harbor, Jackson," Linda whispered menacingly down at me, a smile pulling at the corner of her lips. "And I might just have to talk to them."

Frowning deeply, forcing myself to not let the rage knocking at my gut burst forth, I glared up at her.

"Go away, Linda," I said. "I didn't talk to a reporter in Dubuque."

She stepped back suddenly, as though I'd struck her.

"And I don't intend to," I said cooly. "But if you threaten me—or do anything to jeopardize my business—I will talk to every reporter in every city within two-hundred miles of Head Rock Harbor. Actually, I'll go over there right now, climb up on my mother's bar, and tell everyone about the two dead bodies and how you're threatening me to not tell anyone. And I will make it my personal mission to figure out who is related to those two dead men, and I will have a talk with their families."

Linda's face grew crimson and she shook with anger. Her mouth flapped a few times, she clenched her fists at her side like a toddler, then she stomped away. As she left in her huff, she nearly plowed over Deb, who was exiting the kitchen. My mother turned to watch Linda march out of the restaurant, her husband Mark trailing behind her pitifully. Deb watched the door swing shut, shook her head, and laughed. Then her eyes shot to me. I shrugged.

Looking as suspicious as was appropriate, Deb waltzed over to my table and slid into the booth seat across from me. Folding her arms on the tabletop, she leveled me with her eyes, a sly grin slowly forming on her face. I sat back in my booth and stared back at her.

"What did you do to her excellency?" Deb asked.

"*Excellency* is not a title of respect for a mayor," I said. "Mister, Madam, The Honorable, Your Honor, but—"

"Look here, smarty pants," Deb cut me off. "What did you do to Linda's uppity butt?"

"Nothing," I said. "Truly and surely, for once, nothing. I am completely innocent."

I held my hands out defensively. Deb measured me with her eyes, then sighed and slouched forward.

"As soon as Cleo told me you were here, I told Beau to start up a cheesesteak, rings, and coleslaw," she said.

"Thanks."

"You're welcome. Now, why is Linda looking like someone poured Tabasco on her Tampax?"

My nose turned up on its own. Deb shrugged.

"I don't even...gross, Deb."

"Just tell me what's going on."

I shook my head.

"I'm not supposed to talk about it," I said. "*Even to my cat.*"

Deb's eyebrow raised, but she said nothing.

"But it's best you don't know anyway," I said. "As soon as Pride is over, it won't matter anyway. By the way, I came here to make sure you're all ready for the festivities and don't need anything else from me. That, and lunch."

Deb waved me off. "We're ready. Saturday night will be a hoot. Don't you worry about it."

"Good."

"Now," Deb said, leaning in, "did that have anything to do with the dead guy behind your shop? The *second* dead body this week?"

I jerked back in my seat.

"I thought so," Deb said, nodding.

"How do you know about that?" I whisper-hissed, leaning into the table.

"Everyone knows about the sandbar. Hard to keep that one quiet. But people tend to tell me things," Deb said with a shrug. "Especially when they've had a few beers at my bar."

I frowned at her. Immediately, I went through the list of people who might have stopped at Harper's for a few beers and spilled the beans. The list was short at only four people. All of them worked at or with the police. Unless, of course, one of those people told someone else, and *that person* told Deb. However, from the look on my mother's face, I could tell that if I wasn't going to spill the beans about Linda, she wasn't giving up her informant.

"Word gets around," Deb grinned at me. "You're not the only one who has fun little secrets, sonny boy."

Deacon wouldn't have told my mother what had happened behind my bookstore. Jeremy certainly wouldn't have, either. Marv would have rather been shot dead than go around shooting his mouth off to Deb in the middle of Harper's. Officer Ashley Riley was the only person left. However, I was fairly certain that he was as tight-lipped as Jeremy when it came to police business, especially when Marv was on a tear. He didn't want a target on his butt any more than the rest of us did. Linda and Marv could make his life miserable.

Deb's informant would have to be yet another mystery.

"Where's my food?" I asked.

She stared at me.

"I'm hungry," I said. "May I please have my food?"

"It's still got a few minutes," Deb said, waving me off. "Beau said he'd holler."

I sat back and sighed. Not having any food to distract me and there not being enough customers in the restaurant to distract my mother meant we had no reason not to talk.

"You going to all the events?" Deb asked, the change in subject giving me whiplash.

I looked over at her.

"Well?" she asked again.

"Deacon and I are going to go to the Friday night stuff tomorrow night together," I said. "He asked me to go. So,

I'm taking him as my plus-one to The Dock Saturday night. I got two tickets, so, he invited me to some things, I invited him to others. I figure we'll wander over here for the Rainbow Rave after dinner since I have two tickets to that as well."

"What are you doing?" Deb frowned at me.

I looked around and down at myself.

"What?"

"With that boy?" She shook her head.

"Again," I said, "he's only three years younger than me. We went to high school together. He's not a *boy*."

"Whatever," Deb said. "He's not for you."

"Is that so?" I snorted derisively. "Aren't you the one, not so many months ago, telling me to hurry up and strap some guy down so I could make grandchildren for you or something?"

Deb couldn't help but laugh.

"Yeah," she said. "That sounds like me. But I didn't mean *him*."

"What's wrong with Deacon?" I asked.

Why I was defending my compatibility with Deacon or the appropriateness of our nonexistent relationship was beyond me. I simply didn't enjoy having my mother tell me how to live my own life. Especially since she'd done everything during my childhood to screw it up. If she thought life advice now that I was an adult made up for all of the neglect when I was kid, she was wrong. It was not welcome and it changed nothing about my childhood.

"Nothing," Deb said. "He'll make another guy a lovely partner."

"So?" I asked. "Why am I not that guy?"

"Do you even like the kid?" she asked.

"*Man,*" I said, correcting her again. "Sure. I like him."

"But do you see yourself wanting to *date him*?"

I shrugged.

"Mm." Deb grunted and folded her arms over her chest with a satisfied look.

"What's that even mean?" I grumbled. "*Mm?* Stop acting so high and mighty."

She cackled.

"*Me?* High and mighty? *You,* my dear loin fruit, are calling *me* high and mighty?"

I glowered at her.

"Look," Deb took pity on me, reaching across the table to lay a hand on mine, "Deacon isn't the one. You know it, I know it, this whole town knows it. You seem to want to make things hard for yourself for no reason."

"What are you even talking about?" I snatched my hand away and threw my hands up in frustration. "How am I making things hard on myself?"

"Oh, give it a rest, Jackson," Deb said, sliding to the end of her booth seat. "I know for a fact that Jeremy made the moves on ya'. And you rejected him. For what reason? Get your head out of your rear end and figure things out."

Then she stood and sauntered off to the kitchen. I hadn't heard Beau holler for her, but obviously she was done talking to me. Only two people knew that Jeremy had kissed me in his car after we'd solved how Carter Nelson had died in late spring. Jeremy and me. I hadn't told anyone, and I *knew* Jeremy hadn't told anyone. He wasn't one to admit to being rejected. So, if anyone had spilled the beans to Deb, it had been Jeremy himself.

Maybe over a couple beers at the bar.

It was possible that Jeremy wasn't as tight-lipped with everyone about his work as I thought.

Chapter Thirteen

Early on Friday morning after waking, eating breakfast, and showering, I called Rexie Moynihan over at the fire department. He assured me that he and his crew were clear on the parade instructions and were more than ready to start at 6 p.m. as planned. Hearing the jovial tone from Rexie gave me hope that, at the very least, the first night of Pride Weekend would go well.

After speaking with Rexie, I called Tommy Flint over at the city worker's and sanitation department. I'd spoken to him on Thursday, but I wanted to be certain that they'd have the lights hung for the evening as planned. Reassuring me repeatedly that he already had workers on the task, and that they were far ahead of schedule, I felt the knots in my stomach loosen a bit. After getting off the phone with Tommy, I peeked out the window and saw the city workers securing a string of lights near the lamp post at the corner of the bookstore.

I didn't want to be another burden to the already overworked and overstressed workers at the shops, businesses, and city departments who were helping to pull off a great Pride Weekend. So, instead of making rounds and giving them face time, I shot off texts to everyone to let them know I was available for anything they needed throughout the day, or even the weekend. Most texted back that everything was handled and the others were simply unbothered or too busy to respond.

After making my calls and texts, I noticed I'd had one waiting for me from Deacon.

Confirming that he was going to stop by the shop at five-thirty to attend the parade, feast, and Rainbow Lights together that evening, I responded quickly. Deb's words from the day before were lingering in my head as I tapped out an affirmative. However, I simply couldn't decide if I actually liked Deacon or not. Of course, I *liked* the guy. He was friendly, witty, smart, and fun to be around. I enjoyed his company. However, those words in my head did make me consider whether or not dating him was an actual interest. Was he someone I could consider becoming good friends with, or did I have an actual attraction to him?

Knowing that there was only one way to figure things out, I pushed Deb's voice out of my head for the rest of the morning and afternoon. After going to the Pride Weekend events together that night and then on Saturday, I'd obviously be able to figure things out. If there wasn't some sort of spark with Deacon by Sunday, I'd have my answer. That was the theory I was going to run with, anyway. I'd give Deacon Friday and Saturday to make something inside of me tingle—specifically in places that mattered—and we'd go from there. By Sunday or Monday, I'd either be asking him out to do more things, or I'd make it clear to him that friendship was all I had in mind.

Either way, that didn't clear up anything between Jeremy and me. That was a completely different issue that would have to be addressed at a later time. With everything happening between the two unknown and unnamed men that had been found dead, having even a simple talk about the weather with Jeremy was difficult. Bringing up the kiss in his car and anything he might have possibly said to my mother about it, was a nonstarter.

As that thought entered my head, it was chased away by remembering the two dead men. How did the police not know who the men were yet? Even if neither had any form of identification on them at the time of their deaths, surely, they'd found another way to identify them in the following days? Even if they hadn't, it was unlikely the men—who were obviously out-of-towners—had come to Head Rock Harbor alone for Pride Weekend. Hadn't a friend, boyfriend, or *anyone* shown up at the police department to report them missing? Or called dispatch?

Lila Westbrook hadn't mentioned any guests checking in and suddenly disappearing. If one of her guests had checked in and then simply disappeared, she would have contacted one of the guys, or even Gloria, at the PD. It was as if these men appeared out of thin air, were murdered, and no one knew them, so no one reported them missing. Or, maybe, no one cared that they were missing.

Even more troubling was the niggling thought in the back of my brain. The one I was trying to push out of my head, yet it refused to be evicted. The first victim had looked startling like Deacon. So much so that I'd nearly screamed when I saw the body the first time. The second guy had reminded me of Taylor C. Tomlin, though the resemblance wasn't as close as the one between the first guy and Deacon.

Why did the two victims look so much like people close to me?

A shiver went up my spine. Would the next victim—if there was one—have curly blond hair?

I had to chase that thought out of my head for fear of being creeped out to the point of having to leave my own home to be around people.

But the thought remained there for the rest of the afternoon. If the two murders were connected by a common murderer, then it was possible, maybe even likely, that the murderer would kill again. I was no expert, but I found it hard to believe that someone would kill two people in such a short span of time, then simply dust their hands off and pack things up. The overt violence of the murders also indicated that the murderer was unhinged at best. Someone like that didn't get over their violent tendencies with two murders.

The real and present possibility that someone would be harmed over Pride Weekend made my gut twist up in knots once again. Selfishly, I didn't want anything to ruin all of the hard work that I'd put into organizing the events. I didn't want the business owners and city to have something so important to them ruined. However, I also didn't want innocent people to be harmed by a dangerous individual who, as far as I could tell, had no motive to commit violence. Anyone attending Pride Weekend could be a target for some madman who might simply want to hurt others. No other motivation was needed.

Psychopaths, while rare, exist.

When Rattlesnatches started getting wound up, I had to leave all thoughts of murder aside. In the early afternoon, he knocked all of the books off the A to D shelf of detective mysteries. Then he was randomly tipping books out of the romance section. Finally, he zeroed his focus in on true crime and made a mess of them as well. When I'd finally realized that he was not going to stop being a pain in my neck, I'd scooped him up and taken him up to the apartment. He yowled and hissed as I forcibly removed him from the bookstore, but away he went.

It had been time to get ready for the Parade of Rainbows by that time, anyway. As I showered and coiffed, he scratched at the closed apartment door, making his displeasure known. Ignoring him, I turned on an LGBTQIA playlist, full of bangers, divas, and pop anthems to listen to as I got ready. Either the music soothed the beast or was so gay it beat him into submission, but Rattlesnatches finally settled down. He leapt onto the windowsill next to my bed and busied himself staring at the world outside.

No specific dress code had been given for the Parade of Rainbows Friday evening, as everyone was welcome to show up in whatever made them comfortable. However, I felt that, as the organizer, I should be dressed festively. At least for the first night of Pride Weekend. In the last month, I'd gone to Dubuque and found a fitted white crew-neck t-shirt with a rainbow and "PRIDE" emblazoned on the front. I'd also purchased a rainbow kerchief to tie around my neck. I put on my best jeans, my favorite sneakers, and the t-shirt and kerchief.

If it wasn't clear that I was the organizer of Pride Weekend, it was certainly obvious that I was here, queer, and ready for some cheer. As I was fiddling with the kerchief around my neck, making sure it didn't look like an ascot or styled like something an elderly lady in a T.V. show from the 80s would put around her neck before getting into a convertible, my phone dinged. Glancing at the screen as the phone lay on the bathroom counter, I saw that Deacon had texted.

I'm downstairs!

Smiling to myself, I tapped out a response that I'd be down in a minute.

Once I was certain that I looked acceptable for the evening's events—and, embarrassingly, enticing for my date—I exited the bathroom.

"Okay, you little turd," I said to Rattlesnatches as I slid my phone, wallet, and keys into my pockets. "I'm going out for the evening. If you behave, I'll leave the door open tonight so you can prowl. But right now, you are on punishment. You have to learn how to act like a gentleman with the books."

Rattlesnatches, still posed in the window, turned his head slowly to stare at me. He gave me a disgusted blink of his eyes, turned his nose up, then rolled his head back around to look out the window.

"Sass is not a great start," I said. "Be good while I'm gone."

With that, I turned off the lights in the apartment, leaving the light over the kitchen sink on for Rattlesnatches. As if worried he'd trip on a visit to the potty.

A minute later, I was opening the front door of the shop and stepping out into the warm early evening air and the golden pre-sunset light. Deacon was turned away from the front door of the shop, staring east on Harbor Street as he leaned against the wall of the bookstore, so he didn't notice my arrival. I closed and locked the door, suddenly noticing the swarm of people invading Harbor Street. People lined both sidewalks, were standing in groups in the street and chatting excitedly, and were arriving to the starting point of the parade in droves from all directions.

Rexie Moynihan and Tommy Flint had a few city trucks and one of the fire engines at the west end of the Harbor Street, rainbow bunting draped on the sides, waiting to start. The men and their coworkers were passing out the free rainbow flags on sticks I'd purchased with part of the miniscule Pride budget to anyone who wanted one.

Upon seeing me, several people shouted out excited greetings or waved happily. Of course, this drew Deacon's attention and he pushed way from the bookstore wall and turned to me. A smile lit up his face and he dashed over—I want to say…*gayly*—to greet me. The first thing I noticed was his hair. Having white blond hair to begin with, the dye job he'd done had probably been a breeze, but also temporary. The short hair on the sides of his head was still his natural blond, but the swoop on top of his head that hung over the left side was dyed in streaks of the colors of the rainbow.

Like myself, Deacon had chosen a fitted crew-neck t-shirt with a rainbow on the front. However, his shirt was black, and the word "Pride" was written in white. It was the negative exposure of my shirt. The yin to my yang. He also wore jeans and sneakers, though he hadn't added the flourish of a kerchief. Of course, since I hadn't dyed my hair, I figured we were pretty even on how much we had gayed ourselves up for the first night of Pride Weekend.

"You've been to Dubuque," Deacon said, looking at my shirt with a smile.

"I got it at—"

"Shopko." Deacon chuckled and pulled at the neck of his shirt as he finished my sentence.

The gesture was adorable.

"I believe it," he said. "We both share the trait of enjoying sensible prices."

I laughed.

"Well, I don't have the legs for it or I would have just saved myself the trip and shopped at The Dress Emporium," I replied. "But I have what is often referred to as chicken leg syndrome."

Deacon snorted with laughter and his cheeks looked freshly pinched as he stared into my eyes.

"I don't know," he said casually. "Your legs look pretty good to me."

Refusing to be shy about the compliment, I smiled back and gave him the ole "bro shoulder bump," though I wasn't sure it was the right move. However, he laughed and turned with me to watch the people clamoring for flags at the fire engine. Deacon's arm went around my waist and I felt him hook a finger in the belt loop of my jeans. Obviously, the shoulder check hadn't made him feel less attracted to me. He wasn't so bold to squeeze or grope me, but Deacon's hand held solidly to me, forming to my hip. I didn't mind so much.

In my opinion, the spontaneous physical affection didn't go beyond the bond we'd formed so far.

Once the supply of flags was passed out, Rexie and Tommy announced that the *Parade of Rainbows* would begin. People parted like the Red Sea, clearing the street and taking up positions on either side on the sidewalks. Rexie and his men climbed up into the fire engine and Tommy got into the driver's seat in the city truck at the front of the line. *I'm Coming Out* by Diana Ross—though a little too on the nose for me—began to pour from speakers affixed to Tommy's truck, and the crowd cheered.

Deacon and I shared a glance and a chuckle.

As the trucks slowly started to drive through the crowd, heading east on Harbor Street, we all watched, people in their Rainbow regalia cheering, more than three-quarters waving flags. Out-of-towners stood shoulder to shoulder with locals, cheering and celebrating the opening parade of Pride Weekend.

Since Head Rock Harbor is a tiny little town with no real budget, floats and giant balloons made to look like well-known fictional characters was out of the question. Instead, Rexie and Tommy, and all the city vehicles that could be spared, led the procession, people stepping off the sidewalks once they passed to fall in behind them. The town and its visitors proceeded down Harbor Street, turning south at the corner by the harbor, headed to the square. It would be a short parade—if one could even call it that—but it ended in a city-wide feast.

So, one could say it had a payoff regardless.

Chapter Fourteen

Deciding between brisket, sliced smoked sausage, and pulled pork had me at a stalemate at the barbecue table being manned by Lardell Simmons and Beau and Sawyer Robison. Since I couldn't decide, Lardell snuck a little of each onto my plate. For the payment of five dollars per plate, everyone at the feast was allowed one choice of meat, three sides, a roll, and a soft drink of choice. Water, lemonade, and tea were also available.

However, being the organizer of Pride Weekend came with a few perks. For example, getting a little of each meat available when the person who had made it served it to me. As my date, the perks were extended to Deacon as well. Lardell also gave him a sampling of the trio of meats on his plate, then rushed us along so no one made a big deal about it.

Stick with me, kid. I'd said to him out of the corner of my mouth as we headed to the sides. *I'm going places.*

Once we'd gotten a serving of coleslaw, potato salad, and baked beans, along with a roll, and we'd each grabbed a

Mountain Dew from the trough of iced-down drinks, we found a comfy spot to squat in the grass. Fortunately, as part of the first group to get through the food line, all of the shady spots under the trees weren't taken, so we found prime real estate in the square. Deacon and I had gotten through a fourth of our plates as we chatted with each other and those that sat nearby before everyone had gotten their food.

Once everybody had gotten through the serving line, Mayor Linda Wagner climbed into the bed of one of the city trucks for an announcement. Starting out with thanking everyone for participating in the opening parade of Pride Weekend, she went through the obligatory part of any speech. Yes, Pride Weekend was already a success, which could be seen in the nearly two-hundred people packing the square. She hoped that everyone remained as excited for, and as involved in, the rest of the weekend's activities.

Then, much to my surprise, she announced that one event had to be cancelled due to logistics. The swimming, dancing, and live music that had been planned for early Saturday afternoon at the sandbar had to be taken off of the agenda. Due to the Pride Food and Wine pairings at The Dock that evening, and the Pride Brunch they were hosting the following morning, the sandbar event would interfere. Otherwise, she wished everyone a "Happy Pride" and to enjoy the weekend in a safe and responsible manner.

Shocked that she had taken my advice to at least cancel the event that was to take place at the site of the first murder, I was also relieved. Seeing people celebrating Pride on the site of someone's murder had felt disrespectful to me. Additionally, holding such an event at the murder site could have possibly emboldened the murderer—if he or she was still around. It felt as though a weight had been lifted from my chest.

Deacon must have noticed the change in my demeanor after Linda's speech and everyone got back to eating. He scooted closer in our shaded spot so that our hips were touching while we ate from the plates in our laps. Occasionally, he'd grab and squeeze my knee or shoulder, or lean into me as he spoke so that our sides were pressed together. Again, the physical contact didn't bother me. Nothing he did pushed past what I felt was an appropriate level of contact at this particular section of the "getting-to-know-you" stage.

"I am so full," Deacon said suddenly.

He sat back, propping himself up with his hands in the grass behind him as the plate laid in his lap. Groaning with the food baby obviously brewing in his stomach, he drew a chuckle from me. I was scooping the last forkful of potato salad into my mouth, and being a professional eater, didn't quite return the sentiment. Whether or not there was any dessert had crossed my mind.

"So, should I go see if there's any dessert?" Deacon read my mind, reaching over to pat my knee.

Laughing, I laid my plate atop the one in his lap.

"I could eat some dessert," I said.

"Another drink?" he asked as he started to stand.

"Sure," I said. "Something with less caffeine and sugar, though. "I'm not trying to fly to the moon tonight. I just need to stay awake until the Rainbow Lights are lit."

Deacon chuckled and took our plates and cans and headed off. I watched him walk the several yards to the cans to dump our trash before he headed to the food tables. It occurred to me that I didn't mind the view so much. Between being unbothered by the physical affection he'd bestowed upon me, enjoying his company and banter, and being pleased by the view he provided, maybe my uncertainty was being resolved.

When a person sat down next to me, I was removed from my thoughts, nearly coming out of my skin at the sudden appearance of another human being. Cleo St. Clair, obviously off shift from her job at my mother's bar, was sitting cross-legged next to me, grinning. She had on her typical black jeans, black boots, and a black tank top. Her numerous piercings gleamed in the dying summer sunlight, and her black hair looked nearly blue, it was so dark. However, she held up her arm to show the rainbow bandana tied around her wrist.

"I dressed up," she said simply.

I laughed. "I can see that. Good job."

"I would never disrespect my people by not tagging myself for the queer shindig," Cleo quipped. "Did you already eat?"

I nodded. Curiosity pulled at my brain, since I had never heard Cleo mention her queerness before. However, I kept my questions to myself. Regardless of her sexual identity, there was never a world where I would personally need to know. It did occur to me that, if I were a person to stereotype people, Cleo definitely presented as some flavor of queer. Assuming she was straight simply because she was a pretty woman who worked in my mother's bar had been my fault.

"Mom let you off for the night due to your credentials?" I teased.

Cleo laughed.

"Everyone is off tonight," she replied, waving her hand to cool herself off a bit before popping the tab of her soda. "Since Beau volunteered to cook and serve with Lardell and Sawyer, and then having to get ready for the Rainbow Rave tomorrow night, it only made sense to give everyone the night off tonight."

My eyes grew wide with barely suppressed humor.

"Not even the bar is open?" I gasped.

Cleo laughed at my expression.

"Nope," she said, stretching her legs out.

"Head Rock Harbor will never recover," I teased. "I bet Bernie is doing a landmark business."

"It'll be the only place to sit down and have a drink until tomorrow night," Cleo agreed. "I bet he's absolutely fuming about the tourists."

"He probably has a bouncer at the door checking IDs—not for age, but for place of origin."

We both laughed and Cleo took a long slug of her drink.

"Where is my mother?" I asked, looking around.

"Inventory and other stuff," Cleo replied. "She's at Harper's. She said the feast wasn't really her thing."

"She didn't want to face all the folks who are mad that she's got the bar closed down for the night," I said. "That, and she can smoke inside all she wants and no one will fuss."

Cleo gave me a smile that told me all I needed to know.

"You going to watch the Rainbow Lights after this?" Cleo asked.

Nodding, I looked around for Deacon. He was standing by the coolers, talking to Lardell about something. He glanced over his shoulder as he was speaking, saw me watching him, and smiled. I smiled back and turned my attention to Cleo.

"Yeah," I said.

"Wanna walk over together when it's time?" she asked.

"Oh," I replied, "I'm here with…Deacon."

Cleo rolled her eyes. "I didn't mean as a date."

Laughing, I said, "I know you didn't mean *that*. I just meant, that you'd be joining both of us if you want someone to walk with."

Cleo considered that for a moment.

"Nah," she said. "I don't want to fifth wheel it. Besides, sounds like you two *are* on a date."

I shrugged. "Yeah. I'd qualify it that way. You're probably right. Inviting someone to join us probably won't win me points with him. I mean, this is a community event and we're bound to have people involved in the date in some way, but inviting someone to walk with us everywhere is probably pushing the limit."

Cleo gave me a wink.

"Your mom says you can't be taught anything, but here we are."

"Just because I don't listen to the things she tries to teach me doesn't mean I can't be taught," I quipped. "Tell her that next time she mouths off."

Cleo started to stand, chuckling as she did.

"I'm staying out of y'all's business," she said. "Thanks for the chat. And the rejected invitation to join you."

Amused, I gave her a nod, and Cleo strolled away, right as Deacon returned, a plate in hand and two sodas tucked under his arm. Nodding and smiling at each other as they went opposite directions, Deacon eased himself down next to me. He passed me a can of soda from under his arm, cool water droplets sliding down my hand as I accepted it. The side of his shirt had a round wet ring from the cans, but I assumed the cool water on his side in the warm weather was the least of his worries.

"Well, I managed to get this for us," Deacon said, presenting the plate and two fresh forks.

A nearly quarter of a pie sized slice of apple pie sat on the plate, along with two fresh forks.

"Looks delicious," I said, reaching for one of the forks.

"Lardell made it," Deacon said, taking his utensil. "Straight from Munchies."

Smiling, I dug into the tip of the pie and hurriedly brought the bite to my lips. Deacon followed my lead, taking a larger bite for himself. Seeing that he was not going to pretend to be demure to impress me, I dropped the act. The second dig with my fork produced a much larger bite.

"Cleo seemed to be alone," Deacon said casually. "Maybe we should invite her to walk over with us to the Rainbow Lights later?"

Shrugging, I dug into the pie again and said, "Well, since this is a date, I figured it would be rude to invite someone along."

Deacon grinned widely at me as I slipped the larger bite of the pie into my mouth.

"Want me all to yourself?" he teased.

I nudged him with my shoulder.

"Watch it," I said. "If your head gets much bigger, you'll topple over."

"Funny," Deacon said, digging into the pie once more.

I followed his lead.

"No one's ever complained about my head before," he said.

Somehow, I managed to not spit out the bite of pie.

Chapter Fifteen

There'd been no point in pomp and circumstance in a town the size of Head Rock Harbor. Once the sun was set and twilight was upon us, the feast came to an end and everyone began to walk enthusiastically—yet sluggishly, due to all of the full bellies—back to Harbor Street. Twilight was upon us and nighttime was rapidly swinging in the way it only seems to do in summer. One moment the sun is setting and everything is golden, and the next the street lights are flickering on and the lightning bugs are swarming the violet-colored world.

I'm not certain what the exact protocol is about looking at other men when one is one a date—especially with a cute man. However, as we walked to Harbor Street, it didn't escape my notice that many of the out-of-towners who had settled in Head Rock Harbor for the weekend weren't bad on the eyes. Due to the community feeling of the night's events, everyone was fully dressed. Many of the tourists were wearing the skimpiest muscle tank tops possible, though.

Trying to have a sense of propriety, I did my best to keep my eyes for Deacon and other things.

When I caught his eyes flickering here and there from time to time, I took my chance to check out the out-of-towners, as well. Of course, whether it was intentional or not, it was difficult to not look at an attractive man's barely covered pecs. Even though they were all obviously queer men, many of the women from town couldn't keep their eyes to themselves. Even the queer women who had flooded into town were giving the townies something to rest their eyes on. Fortunately, the tourists didn't seem to mind the attention—not that anyone was being overtly brazen with their stares.

By the time we'd reached Harbor Street, a sliver of dark blue was showing at the horizon, but the sky overhead was velvet and the stars were twinkling down upon us. Nearly two-hundred people packed the length of the street as Tommy Flint pulled one of the city trucks up to the east end corner of town. Deacon and I had settled on leaning against the wall of Head Rock Harbor Books near the east end of the building, by the lamppost. We had a clear view down the street to the truck and we weren't pressed into the street with everyone else like sardines.

As Marv climbed up onto the bed of the pickup to give a speech and announce the Rainbow Lights, Deacon reached down and grabbed my hand. I looked down as his fingers twined through mine. When we both looked up at the same time, he smiled at me and I returned the look. I hadn't planned any physical affection with Deacon when we'd made plans, but he was giving just the right amount of unplanned physical affection. I gave his hand a squeeze and let our arms fall between us lazily as our fingers kept us locked together.

The crowd, boisterous and satiated from the feast, took a moment to quiet down as Marv stood in the bed of the city truck, gesturing for silence. As the crowd quieted down— the tourists taking a bit longer than the townies—Tommy Flint passed Marv a bullhorn. He gave the button a preemptive button-push test, producing feedback, then brought it to his mouth.

"For those of you not from Head Rock Harbor, I'm Chief Marvin Bucksworth—police chief of our stellar police department."

Deacon and I exchanged a look and grinned. When we noticed a few other townies sharing the same look with buddies, we had to keep ourselves from laughing.

"I'd like to say 'hello' to all our citizens of Head Rock Harbor that are in attendance, and 'welcome' to all the new faces we see from out of town. The start of Pride Weekend has been a success and we're excited for the events over the next two days."

A smattering of claps and hoots went off through the crowd.

"Before we light things up here on Harbor Street, I want to give thanks to the people who have made this weekend possible for us. First and foremost, to our city council and Mayor Linda Wagner for finding the budget and getting the ball rolling."

The claps and hoots were sparse, but Marv made a big show of making it seem like the crowd was roaring with approval.

"Also, Tommy Flint and Rexie Moynihan for organizing the city workers to get the infrastructure in place to make Pride Weekend possible."

People were much happier to hoot and clap for the city workers than the leaders of our community.

"The business owners who are hosting events, providing food, and simply being good hosts to our citizens and those of you from out of town also deserve some praise. Not to mention Lardell Simmons and Beau Robison for all the cooking and barbecuing they've been doing for us. And Sawyer Robison for chipping in to help them out where needed."

The three men got the more hoots and clapping.

"A big thank you to Officer Ashley Riley. A lot of us senior men at the department have been running around like chickens with our heads cut off, but he's been pulling extra shifts, throwing in to help wherever and whenever he's needed, even going so far as to run personal errands for the rest of us guys so we can keep things moving smoothly."

Officer Riley got a decent amount of praise from the crowd. Marv's face changed, and I knew he was about to do something he didn't want to do. *Thank me.*

"And lastly, we couldn't have Pride Weekend without the man who organized it for us. He helped all the business owners get ready for Pride, purchased flags and regalia, and helped keep everyone sane through the last several weeks. Everyone give Jackson Harper of Head Rock Harbor Books a big round of applause."

Marv's voice sounded pleasant, but his face told me he would have rather avoided mentioning me if possible. However, when the crowd burst into applause and cheers, many of them turning to find me in the crowd, I simply lifted a hand and gave a simple wave. Deacon squeezed my hand and smiled brightly at me.

"Now," Marv said, quickly directing everyone's attention away from me once again, *"Tommy assured me that we're all ready. So…everyone…welcome to Head Rock Harbor's first annual Pride Weekend. Hit the lights!"*

An electric snap sounded somewhere and, suddenly, the lights that Tommy and the rest of the city workers had strung overhead came to life. In alternating colors of the rainbow, red, orange, yellow, green, blue, indigo, and violet, they'd turned Harbor Street into a tunnel of lights. Each strand, strung from the buildings on one side to wires strung between poles on the other side of the street, created a beautiful rainbow overhead down the length of the street. The crowd roared with cheers as everyone leaned their heads back to take in the lights overhead.

"The Rainbow Lights of Harbor Street, y'all!" Marv announced exuberantly. *"Everyone be safe, be thoughtful, but have fun! Happy Pride Weekend!"*

He began his descent from the bed of the city truck as everyone made noises of wonder at the lights and stood around, gaping like idiots. I stared at the lights for a moment, then turned my head to look at Deacon. He was still admiring the work of Tommy and the boys, so I let my eyes scan the crowd. Everyone seemed pleased with the night's events. They were in awe of the work that had been done with the lights.

Overall, I had to pat myself on the back. Though I hadn't done most of the work, organizing being my role in everything, I was glad to see that the first night had gone off without a problem. Everyone I'd talked to, and organized the evening's events with, had done their part, worked meticulously, and made the night a total success for everyone involved. As long as things kept going the way they were, Pride Weekend would go off smoothly.

I cringed when my eyes fell on Taylor C. Tomlin. He was down by Charlene's Chocolates, standing in the street, looking around at the lights with a couple of men I didn't recognize. I figured he had made friends with some of the other tourists staying at the Inn. I slouched a little, hoping he wouldn't notice me. Not that I assumed he'd be dying to talk to me before he had to on Sunday night, but I didn't want to encourage any interaction beyond what was necessary. From what I'd witnessed the night he arrived, and from what Lila had to say about him, it was in my best interest to keep our contact light.

"Well," Deacon turned to me, still holding my hand, "I guess the evening is coming to an end."

"The lights are lit," I agreed.

I wasn't certain if I was sad that our date was coming to an end, or if I was glad to finally get to go home and snuggle in bed with Rattlesnatches. I'd had a good time with Deacon, and I was happy that we had plans the following day. However, I wasn't certain what that meant. My mother's voice was in my head as I stared at him and held his hand.

"Only the second date," Deacon said quietly as people started up conversations and began milling about around us, "so, no pressure. But do you want to walk me home? Just to delay the inevitable?"

Chuckling, I saw no reason I couldn't delay climbing into bed with Rattlesnatches. The Pride Picnic the following day didn't start until noon. I had plenty of time to get snuggles with my cat, and maybe even watch some T.V., while still having plenty of time for a good night's sleep.

"Sure," I said. "I'd love to."

Deacon beamed at me and turned, pulling me along by my hand. Having his eyes on me instead of where he was going, I wasn't surprised when he bumped into another person. I gave an amused gasp as a person in a black hoodie practically slammed into us, pushing our hands apart as they cut between us down the street. I turned my head to watch the person in the hoodie disappear into the crowd, then, laughing, I turned to Deacon.

"Well, I guess he had somewhere to be," I said with a chuckle.

Deacon was staring down at the sidewalk. My smile slowly melted from my face as I took in my date. I let my eyes move from him to whatever he had spotted on the ground. When my eyes landed on the open pocket knife lying on the cement, my eyes grew wide. When I looked back up at Deacon, I realized he was tugging at the tail of his t-shirt.

When he pulled the fabric to expose the long slash in the material, he looked up at me, his face ashen white.

Not knowing what else to do, I slapped a hand against his side to apply pressure, and screamed for help.

Chapter Sixteen

"Yeah," Deacon said for the hundredth time, though I still didn't believe him, "I really am fine, I promise. I just freaked out at first."

I was standing nearby as Marv oversaw Rexie Moynihan and one of the paramedics employed by the city checking Deacon out. Appearing calm and jovial for those still lingering on Harbor Street, I could practically feel the rage coming off of Marv. If Deacon had actually been cut by the knife, he probably would have been apoplectic. Of course, one more victim might have made the man catatonic. He might have laid down in the middle of Harbor Street and gone into a coma.

Since Deacon was fine and I'd "made a scene" for no good reason, he was simply doing his best to hold back his fury. I couldn't really blame Marv for being upset. I'd screamed fairly loudly for help when Deacon's shirt had been slashed by the guy in the hoodie. We both thought he'd been cut by the knife that lay at our feet. However, after careful examination from me, Marv, and the paramedic—

even Rexie gave Deacon a gander—not a single nick decorated his porcelain skin.

Apparently, the guy in the hoodie had either accidentally sliced Deacon's shirt and dropped his knife…or he hadn't tried hard enough to slice Deacon. My mind was racing with theories about which scenario was most likely to be true. I was chewing at my lip as I considered the fact that the man— *I think it had been a man*—in the hoodie had seem aggressive. It was if he had intentionally bumped into Deacon and me as he pushed his way down the street. Someone who is aggressive and has a pocket knife out and open when pushing through a crowd is most likely looking to hurt someone. At the least, they don't care if they do.

Even if Deacon hadn't been his intended target, he'd been centimeters away from slashing a gash in Deacon's abdomen. Fortunately, the shirt had taken the cut instead. I'd have to send Shopko a written note about the quality of their reasonably priced Pride shirts. Any t-shirt that can protect a person from a knife attack is a good shirt in my mind.

"I think you're right," the paramedic said. "Just shook up, I expect."

Deacon gave a nervous laugh.

"Panic over nothing, I guess," Deacon said.

I tried not to cringe. Though I knew Deacon meant nothing by it and was simply trying to appear unbothered, it was the last thing I wanted him to say in front of Marv. The chief already thought I was trying to cause trouble. Having me scream for help when Deacon wasn't even hurt by the knife the guy in the hoodie had been carrying had only cemented that theory in his head. And, honestly, how could I blame the man? Facts were facts. There had been absolutely nothing to panic over. Deacon was completely fine. Simply shaken up.

Out of the corner of my eye, I saw Marv shoot me a withering look. I kept my eyes on Deacon as he sat on the curb. The paramedic stood and offered a hand to Deacon, which he took and rose to his feet. He muttered a "thanks" and we thanked all the guys who had responded when I'd screeched for help. Once the paramedic and Rexie were gone, I gave him an apologetic smile. He shook his head and smiled, clearly not upset that I had panicked.

Marv, on the other hand, wasn't going to let things go. He stepped over to us as the street around us emptied out, holding the closed pocket knife in one hand. He shook it at me admonishingly.

"You could have started a riot, Jackson," he grumbled, the knife a foot from my face.

"I'm sorry, Marv," I said calmly. "But don't shake that knife in my face."

He squinted angrily and pulled his hand back, realizing that the optics to anyone watching us would have been bad. Deacon sighed.

"I panicked," he said to Marv. "I was grabbing at the slash in my shirt and Jackson did what any decent person would have done if they thought someone had been stabbed. He called for help. Waiting—if I'd been jabbed—could have caused bigger problems."

Marv shot a glower at Deacon, but the anger was beginning to melt from his face.

"Don't blame Jackson for just being worried about me," Deacon said.

I kept my eyes on Marv, wondering if he'd at least listen to Deacon's reasoning.

It took a few moments of him turning the knife round and round, over and over in his hand before he seemed to make up his mind. Finally, he slipped the knife into his pocket and stood to face us both. I wanted to tell him that he had basically destroyed evidence—if the person had actually meant to harm Deacon—but realized it was best to keep that thought to myself.

"You two get on home," Marv said with finality. "And be safe."

Without another word, he turned on his heels and marched away towards the cruiser waiting at the end of the street. Officer Riley was standing by the hood, and when he saw Marv coming, he slid into the driver's seat. Marv hopped into the passenger seat and they took off. Deacon and I watched them drive away, the cruiser turning south at the corner towards the police department.

Once they were out of sight, Deacon turned to me and smiled, shaking his head.

"He gets a fire up his butt over the littlest thing lately," he said.

"Not so little," I said, reaching out to tug at the slash in his shirt. "That could have been really bad."

Deacon shrugged. "Well, I'm fine. So…I guess we should let it go?"

"I guess," I said with a sigh, letting my hand fall back to my side. "Walk you home?"

He grinned. Of course."

"Just so we're clear," I said as we walked west on Harbor Street, "I don't go up to guy's places for a coffee on the second date, either."

Deacon cackled with laughter. "Well, I guess we got enough excitement out of tonight."

"Surely," I said.

"Don't call me *Shirley*," Deacon teased.

Laughing, we walked west on Harbor Street towards Deacon's apartment across town. The trip on foot takes only a few minutes. Nothing in downtown Head Rock Harbor is very far from anything else. From the northernmost end of town to the southern tip of downtown, I can make it in seven minutes at a leisurely stroll. Getting to Deacon's apartment that was less than a quarter mile from the bookstore was a quick trip.

Deacon most likely would have been safe on his own, walking to his apartment. However, I felt that there was power in numbers. If the guy in the hoodie had been intending to hurt him, he might return once he realized Deacon was fine. Even if he hadn't meant to hurt Deacon, and he'd simply dropped the knife, then kept going when he'd realized how things would look, I wanted Deacon to *feel* safe. In the dark of night, walking home on empty streets can always feel a bit dangerous. Even in tiny little river towns.

We hadn't even really had time to start up a solid conversation before his apartment building was coming into view. One of the newer buildings in town—having been built in the last decade—Deacon's apartment building made me feel that he'd be safe inside. The front door required a fob to get into the lobby after hours. All of the apartment entrances were interior, and other than the front and back doors that had security measures in place, there was no other way to get into the individual apartments. Unless you had a grappling hook and excellent climbing skills.

"I'm sorry again," I said, getting in one last apology before our walk ended. "If I embarrassed you the way I freaked out."

Deacon chuckled.

"I would have freaked out if things were flipped. I'm sure I looked panicked, and then there was the cut on my shirt, and…well, don't worry about it. You were the appropriate level of freaked out as far as I'm concerned."

I gave him a grateful smile.

"Thanks," I replied and nudged his shoulder with mine.

"It was just weird, you know?" Deacon mumbled.

"Huh?" I stepped over a crack in the sidewalk.

One should always avoid bad luck and breaking one's mother's back whenever possible.

"I actually thought it was my neighbor again." Deacon chuckled nervously.

"Your neighbor?" I questioned. "Again?"

"Yeah," Deacon shook his head with a smile as we approached the front door of his apartment building. "This new guy who moved into the apartment next door. The guy who broke my phone?"

"What?" I turned to him. "You didn't tell me *someone* broke your phone. You just said it broke and you had to buy a new one."

"I guess I didn't think you would want to hear all the stupid details. Well," Deacon said, "he didn't actually break it. But he slammed into me coming through the door into the stairwell. Nearly knocked me over the railing. Three floors up. It would have been bad. The fact that I dropped my phone over the railing instead was bad enough."

I stared at Deacon, my brow furrowing as I listened.

"He didn't even say 'sorry' or 'excuse me' or 'get bent' or anything," Deacon grumbled. "He just raced down the stairs like he was off for some hot date or something."

He laughed and grinned at me.

"Which I guess I understand," he said. "I'd had a pretty nice date myself right before."

Deacon nudged my arm and I managed to give him a small smile.

"Why did you *think* it was him?" I asked. "Don't you know what he looks like?"

He shrugged. "He's always wearing that hoodie."

"You should go over and introduce yourself," I cocked an eyebrow. "Put a face with the name. In case he thinks he can push you around, he'll think twice next time."

Deacon shook his head comically as he used his fob to unlock the door. We both stepped inside, glad to be out of the warm summer night and into the air-conditioned lobby. I gave the place a quick glance, realizing it was done like most modern apartment buildings. Lots of industrial features, exposed brick and HVAC and whatnot. The rent was probably way higher than it was worth, but seeing as I owned my own place due to inheritance, I wasn't going to judge the rental payments of others.

"No," Deacon said. "He doesn't seem like the type to want to make friends, if you know what I mean."

I laughed. "Well, until tonight, he was carrying a knife on him."

Deacon nodded.

"Anyway," Deacon said, "I'm 3D, and he's in 3E. I think. That's where I think I saw him shoot out of on his way to the stairs. As long as he stays over there, I'll just mind my business."

"Until he cuts another one of your shirts," I said.

Laughing, Deacon nodded. "Until then."

Casting a hopeful wish, I decided to tell Deacon what was swirling in my brain.

"Do you mind if I go up to 3E and see who it is?" I asked. "You know, once you're securely in your apartment and he won't see you so it won't cause problems between you and him?"

Deacon thought it over for a second.

"Well, if I end up dead, it might be good to have a lead," he said.

"Bad joke."

"Sorry." Deacon blushed. "Yeah. That's fine. Come on."

I fell in beside Deacon and he led me to the stairwell. A door at the back of the lobby led to flights of stairs that led up the back of the building to each floor of apartments. Painted metal railings and brick walls met us as we entered and began our ascent. I hadn't seen an elevator in the lobby, but I wanted desperately to ask Deacon if there was one available. Three flights of stairs while carrying groceries had to be rough.

Once we reached the fourth floor—which was technically the third floor, since the bottom floor of the building had no apartments in it—I was nearly out of breath. Being a person who is constantly walking, and even climbing a flight of stairs multiple times a day in my home, three flights of stairs is still three flights of stairs. Doing all that climbing in one go was not in my wheelhouse. Deacon, on the other hand, seemed unbothered.

Grinning when he saw the look of exasperation on my face, he politely said nothing. Instead, he waved me forward and we went through the painted metal door that had "3rd Floor" painted on it in block letters. Out of the stairwell and into the hallway that led to the apartments, I saw that the industrial motif from the lobby carried on upstairs.

Polished concreted floors and exposed brick was everywhere. All of the apartment doors were metal and rough, as though belonging in a warehouse instead of an apartment building. I followed Deacon along the hallway until we got to 3D. At the door, we exchanged a quick hug and reminded each other we had the Pride Food and Wine pairings at The Dock the following night, and then the Rainbow Rave after.

Deacon let himself in his apartment, gave me one last grin over his shoulder, and shut the metal door behind himself. Once I heard the lock click into place, I strolled over to the door marked 3E. Suddenly, I realized it was late in the evening—maybe too late for some people—and it might be poor manners to come knocking at such an hour. I checked my phone and saw that it was barely after ten o'clock, so it shouldn't be considered too rude on a weekend. Worrying about the time had probably been my brain trying to convince me to do the safest thing and run away.

However, my fist rose of its own accord and my knuckles rapped on the metal door. The clanging sound was muffled by the insulated door, but it was loud enough that anyone inside would know they had someone calling. After half a minute, I nearly raised my fist to knock once more, but the sound of shuffling feet and someone groping at the door made me stop. Standing up straight and putting on my best *I mean business* face, I waited for the door to slide back.

When the door slid away and I was looking down at an elderly woman in a house coat, her hair up in curlers, and her glasses perched precariously at the tip of her nose, my stern expression melted. She looked as if she had fallen asleep in front of the T.V. and had roused herself to see which rude person had come knocking on her door so close to bedtime. She stared up at me like a mole freshly out of the burrow, adjusting its eyes to the sun.

"I'm so sorry," I said immediately. "I think I have the wrong apartment."

"Oh?" the woman squeaked. "Who are you looking for, baby?"

"I'm not sure," I said, having to laugh. "I thought a man lived here. About so high—"

I motioned with my hand to indicate that the man was a little taller than me.

"—wears a black hoodie a lot. I think youngish?" I finished.

Even I knew that my description of the man and the way I presented the information was suspicious. Anyone my age would assume I was looking to buy drugs. Fortunately, the elderly woman took my confusion at face value.

"No," she said slowly, sincerely thinking about it, "I've lived here since they opened the place up, hun. I'm sorry."

"No, no," I said waving her off. "It's late and I obviously made a mistake. I'm so sorry."

She grinned. "Don't you worry about it at all. I don't get a wide variety of visitors, so it's nice to see a new face now and then. I was living out there at the apartments on the highway? By the Casey's? Well, they were getting old and keeping up with everything was getting to me, so I was going to go up to Dubuque to be in a rest home. That's where my daughter is?"

I nodded along, as if this woman telling me her life story was normal and warranted.

"But then they built this place and they were talking up how easy they'd be to keep clean with all the sleek features, how they're close to everything in town. *You can walk anywhere*, they'd said. Even had a discount for seniors, service people, and the disabled. So, you betcha I was one of the first. Been here six-seven years now, I guess? Love it. Good to stay near family, too. You looking for a place?"

"No," I chuckled. "I have a place. An apartment. I own Head Rock Harbor Books and live above it."

"Oh!" the woman exclaimed and reached out to nudge me excitedly. "I've been telling myself for forever I need to stop by and get some books. Now that I know the owner—what did you say your name was?—I'll definitely have to."

"Jackson," I said. "Harper. Jackson Harper."

I reached out my hand. The woman slid hers into mine and shook it vigorously.

"Annetta Bowles," she said. "Not *Anita, Annetta*."

"It's nice to meet you Ms. Bowles," I said. "Come by the shop anytime. We reopen with a new coffee bar on site on Tuesday. I might even manage a discount for seniors, too."

Ms. Bowles slapped at my arm happily.

"You can bet I will now!" she said. "I'm sorry I don't know this fellow you're looking for."

"You get back to what you were doing," I said, waving her off. "I was obviously mistaken."

Ms. Bowles beamed at me and stepped back inside her apartment, slowly shutting her door.

"Nice to meet you, baby," she said as the door closed.

"Same to you," I said as the door closed.

Ms. Bowles locked the door audibly behind her and I sighed, turning to face the hallway down to the stairs. As I walked down the hall, I pulled out my phone and started to tap out a message to Deacon. Letting him know that he was confused about his next-door neighbor so that he wouldn't be wondering what I found out was the right thing to do. As I approached the stairwell, I stopped suddenly, noticing an alcove to the right. Glowering, I finished my message to Deacon.

An older lady named Annetta Bowles lives next door to you. No guy in a hoodie. There's an elevator in a hidden alcove by the stairwell.

I had pushed the button for the elevator and was stepping inside when the response came.

I figured if we weren't going to get physical, we could still get exercise.

Laughing, I shook my head and slid my phone into my pocket as the elevator closed.

Chapter Seventeen

The Mississippi waters were calmer than usual, which meant that the wind was virtually nonexistent. Sawyer and I were staked out at one of the picnic tables at the harbor, passing out rainbow-colored candy to kids and adults alike. Anyone who wanted lollipops, gummies, or sour chewy bites of sugar was stopping by to snag one of the free Pride Swag Bags of candy. With some of the budget, I'd ordered plenty of rainbow-colored, fruit-flavored candy and cellophane bags with rainbow twist ties. Sawyer, being the nice guy that he was, had volunteered to put the bags of candy together and pass them out on Saturday afternoon during the picnic.

Since I hadn't wanted to go to the picnic and potentially face Marv once more, I'd sauntered over to the harbor to help Sawyer. I'd put together a picnic basket for us, though he hadn't asked me to, since he hadn't known I was coming to join him. However, he was grateful to see that he wasn't going to miss out on lunch with the job he'd volunteered to do. Within fifteen minutes, we'd passed out all the free candy and everyone had wandered over to the square to join the picnic with their lawn chairs, blankets, coolers, and baskets.

Even sitting at the picnic table down by the harbor, the two of us could hear the celebration at the square. Jimmy Buffet was drifting on the barely-there breeze. *They probably put on* Boats, Beaches, Bars, and Ballads *to please locals and tourists alike,* I thought to myself. I wasn't sorry I wasn't a part of it. Sawyer seemed unbothered as well.

Of course, when you're digging your teeth into a mile high roast beef sandwich with all the trimmings, it's hard to be upset. I'd made sandwiches for both of us, packed some chips, a few chocolate chip cookies apiece, and a few sodas. I'd brought a couple apples as well, so we could pretend part of our meal was healthy.

"So, what do you think?" I asked.

Sawyer chewed the bite currently in his mouth, swallowed, and gave me a nod.

"It's good," he said. "You make a mighty fine sandwich." Then he winked.

"I mean about what I asked you," I chuckled and popped a chip in my mouth.

"Which part?" he asked, stuffing the last bite of his sandwich into his mouth.

"My theory about the murders," I said, leaning in to mutter.

There wasn't anyone around, but I certainly didn't want anyone overhearing us. If anything got back to Marv or Linda, my goose would be cooked. Even though I was only confiding in Sawyer, it would still look bad. They'd say I was *stirring up trouble* or *riling up the populace* or something. Before you knew it, they'd claim I was starting a militia to overthrow the local government. So, keeping things as quiet as possible, even talking to Sawyer, was best.

Sawyer looked around comically, proving how ridiculous it was that I was whispering.

"Linda and Marv already have it out for me," I said. "I'm just being careful."

"And you're not worried I'll say something to them?" Sawyer asked, sitting back and popping the tab of a Mountain Dew he'd fished out of the basket.

"No," I said. "You're a good friend. And a good guy."

"Good guy, huh?" Sawyer sipped his drink and looked thoughtful, not making eye contact. "Then why do I hear you're hanging out with Deacon Davis? Word on these streets is that Jeremy Morris might be making sweet on you, too. *Finally.*"

"Cheese and rice," I muttered. "Does everyone in this town know what's going on in my love life?"

Sawyer gave me an amused smile, but there was bitterness behind it.

"You know," I said, "you never actually asked me out. So…you snooze you lose."

"What if I did?" he asked. "Asked you out?"

"I would have accepted a date," I said, thoughtfully. "But it wouldn't have worked out."

He looked confused, maybe a little hurt.

"You're a river rat," I said. "You're an outdoorsy guy. You'd get tired of my prissy ways pretty quickly, man. But as a friend, you could tolerate me."

He stared at me for a moment then a laugh erupted from his throat.

"You got me there," Sawyer said jovially. "Can't see myself settling down with someone who's afraid to get dirty."

I laughed. "My point exactly."

"Well, the right guy or gal will come along eventually," he said with a sigh. "I guess I won't hold any ill will towards you. As long as your cat doesn't maul me on my next visit to the bookstore."

"It happened once!" Laughter launched the response from my throat.

Once we settled down, I gave Sawyer a solid look.

"So?" I asked. "What do you think?"

He looked thoughtful again as he sipped at his soda.

"It would make sense," he said. "That some homophobe is attacking people *because* of homophobia. Pride Weekend and all. Tourist at the sandbar. Tourist behind your shop. Deacon's gay. That could explain it. Doesn't really help figure out who it is, though. Most people around here are tolerant, even if they have some biases."

"And the real racists and homophobes tend to keep it quiet," I said.

He tipped his soda at me and winked, then took another sip.

"The guy in the hoodie," Sawyer asked, "was he young? Old? White? Black?"

"I'm not even certain it was a guy," I said, shaking my head. "Though probably. Little bit taller than me. Probably not a woman. If it was, it's an out-of-towner because no women in Head Rock Harbor are over six foot. That I can think of. Well, Betty Wickshaw was taller than me, but she's dead, so…"

"I can't think of one, either," Sawyer said. "So, probably a guy. A hoodie, to me, says *younger*. Old men don't really rock hoodies around here. They're more into the Carhartt. And the demographics alone…it's most likely a white guy."

"Agreed," I said. "Most serial murderers are, anyway."

Sawyer grinned.

"But he doesn't live in the apartment Deacon thought he was coming out of?" he asked.

"Nope. Little old lady. Uh, Annetta Bowles. Yeah."

"Don't know her," Sawyer said.

"Me, either," I replied. "But she said she used to live out at the apartments on the highway by Casey's? A lot of people from miles away moved into those over the years because they were cheap. Older woman on a fixed income? She could've been lured there from any of the smaller towns around here. But I didn't ask her where she was originally from. Said her daughter is in Dubuque."

"A lot of folks around here are from or have moved to Dubuque," Sawyer said. "Those of us originally from here are getting fewer and fewer."

Sawyer made a humming noise as he thought and sipped his soda. I popped the tab on mine after pulling it from the basket and put on my tightest thinking cap as well. After a few moments, it was obvious that neither of us were any closer to figuring out who might be behind the stabbing murders. Even getting a glance at the guy at the Rainbow Lights—if that had even been the suspect—didn't help us any.

As I was about to say something to Sawyer, I noticed a police cruiser out of the corner of my eye. I turned my head slightly to see it turning south at the Harbor Street corner.

Jeremy was behind the wheel and Officer Riley was in the passenger seat. When Jeremy realized I'd noticed him looking over at Sawyer and me, he gave me a tight smile, though it didn't reach his eyes. Sawyer and I both smiled back and waved.

Then Jeremy continued on down the street, away from the harbor.

"He's got it out for you," Sawyer whistled before chuckling.

"What?"

"That was pure passion and annoyance in those eyes, man," Sawyer said. "Everyone knows he's not happy that you're dating Deacon. He may be your friend and letting you do what you think you need to do, but he's jealous."

I turned my head back to stare at Sawyer.

"Green, man," Sawyer said with an amused nod. "Envy to the core."

"*Everyone* knows?" I frowned. "Everyone in town knows my business?"

"Well," Sawyer said, "maybe not everyone. But those of us that have known you two well for long enough, I guess?"

Shaking my head, I took another sip of my drink.

"I'm not going to date Jeremy just because everyone expects me to," I grumbled.

Sawyer snorted with laughter.

"What?" I barked, irritated. "Just because Jeremy and I grew up together and…all that stuff…people think we're, I don't know, Romeo and Juliet?"

"Oof," Sawyer said. "I'd have chosen lovers who weren't so star-crossed. And were alive at the end."

I couldn't help but laugh.

"The way things are going," I said, "who knows?"

Sawyer laughed wickedly and tapped his soda can against mine. As he started to rise from the picnic table, I started packing up our trash and utensils, making sure to swipe leftover crumbs into the grass for the critters. Once I had the basket packed away, I slid out of the table and joined Sawyer at the end to stare out at the river.

"You know," Sawyer said, "I like you, Jackson. Maybe we were never meant to date, but somehow, I'd feel better losing the opportunity to Jeremy. Losing it to Deacon just doesn't feel right."

"What an odd thing to say to a friend," I said, teasing him.

He chuckled. "You know what I mean."

I chewed at my lip, but didn't respond.

"If you're kind of sweet on someone, being rejected doesn't hurt so much when they end up with someone they're obviously meant to be with," Sawyer said. "That's all."

"*Meant to be* sounds so weird," I groaned pitifully.

"You can qualify it however you want," Sawyer said, finishing his drink and handing me the can to throw away. "But I always found it odd, Jeremy chasing all the tail that came through this town. You not saying anything about it. The two of you acting like you're just best friends. We all know where this is headed."

"Down the drain," I said.

Sawyer nudged me with his shoulder and smiled at me.

"All right," he said. "I see how you're going to be."

He turned and started to walk towards Harbor Street. I went over to the trash can to empty the trash from the basket.

"If you and Jeremy want to keep acting simple," Sawyer said, getting my attention, "go on ahead. But seems like gay guys are dropping like flies around here. You might want to figure things out before it's too late."

Rolling my eyes at the bad joke, I waved him off.

"Don't be a stranger, though," Sawyer said. "We're definitely friends. We can still hang out and do friend things. Right?"

"Absolutely," I said.

I jaunted over to join him and we carried on walking towards Harbor Street.

Chapter Eighteen

With the cancellation of the live music and dancing that had been planned for Saturday after the picnic, we had a gap in our Pride Weekend schedule. Fortunately, this gave me time to get back to the shop after having lunch with Sawyer so that I could open for a bit during the Tour the Shops of Harbor Street event. Since Deacon and I had plans to go to the Pride Food and Wine Pairings event at The Dock at six o'clock, I planned to keep the shop open from four until five so that locals and tourists alike could come in and look around.

For a solid hour, there was a stream of people winding through the shop, looking at the books, the new coffee bar that was built, and giving Rattlesnatches scratches behind his ears. He laid in the front window majestically, and graciously accepted all of the attention until five o'clock. Once I'd chased everyone out of the shop, stating how much I regretted having to get ready for the dinner at The Dock, I ran upstairs.

Grabbing a quick shower, I primped and coiffed for my dinner date with Deacon. Doing the best I could, I knew that summer evenings on the river could quickly turn humid. No matter what I did with my curls, their fate was really in God's hands. However, I tamed them the best I could before putting on all the things that helped me stay smelling pretty throughout the day. I slipped into a pair of slacks, some dress socks and shoes, and a button-down long-sleeve shirt.

After a bit of deliberation, I decided that a tie was appropriate and required for a fancy prix fixe dinner at The Dock. At the back of my closet, I found a tie I probably hadn't worn since my university graduation, but worked for the outfit. I had to shake it out a bit and spritz it with some cologne to liven it up, but it looked fine once I remembered how to actually tie it around my neck. When I finally took a look in the mirror, I felt I'd made myself up nicely for the date.

When Deacon arrived a little before six, he had smartly brought his car. I slid into his shiny, but unassuming, silver Honda Civic, glad we wouldn't be walking to The Dock in our nice clothes in the humidity. The possibility that my curls might make it through dinner had me feeling better than I'd felt before I started organizing Pride Weekend. As he drove us over to The Dock, Deacon rested his hand on my thigh, giving it a squeeze as he smiled and drove.

Again, I found myself feeling as though he wasn't pushing past any established boundaries for physical affection. A thigh squeeze on the third date was certainly nothing to ruffle any feathers over. However, I found that his hand on my thigh didn't feel as intimate as it should have. It didn't make me uncomfortable the way that Jeremy did when he touched my knee or thigh. At first, I thought that maybe that meant that I was much more comfortable with Deacon than I was with Jeremy, and my answer to my conundrum was before me.

When it occurred to me that I felt comfortable with Deacon touching me because there was no risk of the physical affection being returned on my end, my stomach sank. I didn't get worked up over Deacon touching me because there was no danger behind the affection he bestowed upon me. It was like a friend showing affection—not a potential lover. Whenever Jeremy touched me, my body was sending up warning signals.

Behave yourself or this will become indecent.

By the time I was sliding out of the passenger door of Deacon's car in the packed parking lot of The Dock, I felt sad. By the end of the weekend, I'd need to make my intentions clear with Deacon. I didn't want to ruin the Pride Weekend for him, so I decided that once everything was over, I'd say something. In the meantime, I'd make sure to shrug off any physical affection that felt romantic. A quick hug was okay, but hand holding and thigh squeezing were definitely off the table. If he tried to play footsie at dinner, I'd stomp his toes.

Not really. But I'd definitely not engage.

So, it was no surprise that Deacon was confused when I dodged his hand when he went to grab mine as we walked towards the entrance to The Dock. I played it off as though I hadn't noticed he was reaching for my hand, excited to get to dinner. By the time we were inside with the throngs of people with tickets to the special dinner, Deacon looked as if he'd forgotten all about it. The hostesses were doing their best to seat people quickly, but it was easy to tell that it would be a minute before they got the horde squared away.

"*I'm going to hit the head,*" Deacon whispered in my ear. "*If they seat you before I'm done, I'll come find you.*"

"*I'll just wait by the bar,*" I said back. "*That way we don't risk losing each other.*"

"*Okay,*" he said. "*I'll come find you there and then we'll come back here to get seated.*"

I gave him a smile and a nod, and he disappeared into the crowd towards the bathrooms. Squeezing between people, giving polite nods and thanks as I made my way, I finally found my way out of the group by the front doors and headed over to the bar. Already flooded with orders coming from seated tables, the bartender gave me a harried nod. I gestured, indicating that I wasn't waiting to be served, which drew a look of relief from him, causing me to chuckle.

I turned and propped an elbow up on the bar and stared out at the massive dining room. The floor-to-ceiling windows at the far end of the restaurant looked out on the outside seating and the river just beyond. Looking around the room, I was glad I had dressed more formally than I typically did. Nearly all of the other patrons had chosen dresses, skirts, suits, and the like. Deacon and I would have stuck out like a sore thumb if we'd come casual.

When I accidentally caught the eye of Linda Wagner, sitting in a cozy corner with her husband, I turned towards the bar so she wouldn't catch the sour look that overtook my face. Fortunately, we had no reason to talk to each other, so her at one end of the restaurant, and me at the other, kept me safe from any interaction. I'd just have to make sure that the hostess didn't seat us near her table if at all possible. As I considered how much I might have to tip to make that certain, someone slid up to the bar next to me.

Turning my head to see if Deacon had come to find me, I found myself staring up into Jeremy's eyes instead. He was smiling awkwardly down at me as he leaned against the bar. As everyone else had done, he'd shown up to the dinner in his finest slacks, button-down shirt, tie, and dress shoes. I gave him a once over, and when my heart fluttered, I became immediately angry with myself. Hoping it didn't show on my face, I smiled at him.

"Here alone for the dinner?" Jeremy asked.

"No," I said. "Deacon's in the bathroom. Waiting on him before we go get seated."

Jeremy's face became a blank slate and he nodded.

"You?" I asked, looking around. "Bring a guy?"

Jeremy shook his head. "I was going to bring Ashley, but he's got family stuff. So, I brought Gloria as my plus-one."

"Well, he's married and straight," I shrugged. "But it was nice of you to bring Gloria. Tickets were hard to come by."

Jeremy gave me a nod. "He's not with his wife. Other family stuff, I think."

"What?"

"Ashley. He's not—it doesn't matter," Jeremy chuckled. "I just meant I didn't get turned down for a woman. That would never happen."

I couldn't help but chuckle at that.

"But I guess cute little twinks are competition," Jeremy added casually, swallowing the tail-end of the sentence as though I might miss it.

"Excuse me?" I cocked an eyebrow at him.

"Deacon," Jeremy said with a sigh. "He's going to be a problem."

Rolling my eyes and pushing away from the bar, I stood to face Jeremy, lacing my arms over my chest. Hopefully, I didn't look too aggressive to anyone paying attention to us. However, I suddenly found myself filled with frustration for my best friend. If I could even call him that anymore.

"Okay," I said. "Drop the crap, Germ. The jealousy act is getting old."

He stared at me passively, trying his puppy dog eye look once more.

"That doesn't work on me," I said. "I'm not one of your boy toys with more abs than brains."

Jeremy frowned at me, the look immediately disappearing.

"And," I said, "you know what? It's not a good look. Going around being jealous. People are noticing."

"Who's noticing?" Jeremy frowned at me. "Noticing *what* exactly?"

"This pining for your best friend who you're supposed to end up with because we're both gay and have known each other forever thing." I explained. "Apparently, the whole town's-a-talkin'. Of course, you going to Harper's at night and getting sideways and laying your heart out to my mother doesn't help things, either."

"What?" Jeremy laughed heatedly.

"You. My mother."

"*Sideways?*" Jeremy grumbled angrily. "Is that what she says about me? I'm coming to Harper's and getting...*sideways*? How is the town's second most infamous drunk going to say that about me?"

Jeremy realized what had come out of his mouth a moment too late. I stared up at him, one brow raised. We stood in silence for a moment, simply staring at each other.

"Watch your mouth," I said finally.

My mother—and everyone in town knew it—was an alcoholic in recovery. And sometimes her recovery journey took her through some seedy neighborhoods. I could call her a drunk or anything else I wanted—because I'd grown up with her and had the battle wounds to prove it. I'd done several tours of duty. Jeremy, and everyone else, had no right to speak about Deb Harper the way that I could if I chose to—though I never did.

"I'm sorry. I shouldn't have said that," Jeremy said, and I could tell he meant it. "But your mother shouldn't be going around talking about me. Or you. And it's not like it's not true, either."

"You are walking a thin line right now," I said quietly as I stared up at him.

"Oh, come on, Jacks," Jeremy said. "If it weren't for your Aunt Belinda, you'd be—"

"Just cut it out," I cut him off. "Stop acting a fool and giving the town things to talk about. And keep your thoughts about Deb to yourself."

"*Deb?*" Jeremy laughed bitterly. "You call your mom by her first name. You don't realize how weird that is?"

"I call her 'mother' sometimes. Or 'mom'," I sputtered, then stopped myself. "Why am I even explaining myself to you? Just stop whatever it is you're doing. And stop talking to *my mom*."

Seeing Deacon coming our way over Jeremy's shoulder, I stepped away.

"Enjoy your dinner," I said curtly.

Jeremy, not to be dismissed, wrapped a hand around my forearm. When I turned to glare at him, he levelled me with his eyes.

"I haven't been out drinking at Harper's since I saw you last Saturday," he said firmly. "We were gone before you and Deacon, too. And I haven't said a word to your mother about…*anything*."

We stared at each other for a moment, a confused furrow digging its way into my brow. Finally, as Deacon approached, Jeremy let his hand slip from my arm.

"Are we ready to get a seat?" Deacon asked evenly, his eyes on Jeremy, though he was speaking to me.

"Yeah," I managed to say. "Let's…go get seated."

"Sounds good," Deacon said, lacing an arm around my back and pulling me away. "Jeremy."

He nodded over his shoulder at Jeremy as we walked away.

"Deacon," Jeremy said, but with my back turned, I couldn't see what kind of snarl he gave my date.

Chapter Nineteen

By the time we got to the Rainbow Rave at Harper's, the party was in full swing. Of course, Deacon and I had spent three hours enjoying the three courses and three glasses of wine at The Dock. Even though the knowledge that I was going to let him down easy by the end of the weekend filled my head, he was still great at conversation. Laughing and telling stories, we enjoyed the salad course, the steak and sides as the main, and the tiramisu with berries served at dessert. The chardonnay with salad was crisp and refreshing. The merlot served with the main was peppery and dry, and the sparkling sweet wine served with dessert was perfect to end the meal.

Rolling out of The Dock with the last of the diners, Deacon and I were exuberant and ready to party. Against our best judgment, he drove us down to the bookstore, where I ran inside and changed into clothes more appropriate for Harper's and the Rainbow Rave. Then we stopped at his apartment where he ran upstairs, changed, and got back to the car in a timeframe that seemed super human. Of course, with three glasses of wine in me, time had begun to mean nothing.

Racing over to Harper's Bar, Grill, Bait & Tackle, Deacon and I found another full parking lot. People had even spilled out of the building to dance and hang out in the parking lot. It was obvious having a ticket to the event meant nothing. Everyone was simply showing up. As Deacon and I hopped from his car to go inside, I noticed Marv stationed in a cruiser near the Harper's sign, watching the crowd warily. Another cruiser was across the lot, and Jeremy was seated on the hood, keeping an eye on the crowd. Apparently, he'd been off duty for dinner, but he was expected to help Marv keep the rowdy partiers in check at Harper's afterward.

Serves him right, I thought to myself. The fact that Jeremy couldn't be in Harper's checking out all the guys—*during a Pride Weekend*—felt like karma.

Talk about my mother, you don't get to chase tail during tail chasing season, punk.

Once we'd pushed through the boisterous crowd outside, made up mostly of the locals trying to avoid the out-of-towners inside, we headed straight to the bar. With the side effects of the wine threatening to slip away, Deacon and I agreed more booze was needed. Deb had made her staff remove all of the tables and chairs from the restaurant side of the building. The booths were still available for seating, and the stools in the bar were still in place, but it was standing room only for the most part.

Obviously, Deb had wanted there to be more room to dance to the music that was thrumming through the place. The rainbow laser lights she'd had put up for the occasion were whipping over the heads of the crowd. Glow necklaces shone around necks throughout the crowd and glow sticks were waving in the air as some pop song I didn't recognize blared from the speakers. If I had to guess, it was something by a singer named Gaga, or Ariana, or something similar. When it came to music, I wasn't up to date on what the young gays like myself were enjoying.

Regardless, I dance-walked with Deacon through the crowd to the bar area. It took some squeezing and pushing and making polite excuses, but we finally found ourselves standing at the bar to order. Cleo spotted Deacon and I immediately, and she ignored everyone to come over to us. Since Sawyer was behind the bar helping her out—our man of all trades—it wasn't like everyone else had to wait for us. As she approached us from the other side of the bar, Beau slid in behind the bar to help out. I supposed since food wasn't being served during the party, it made sense that Beau moved from cook duties to bartender duties for the evening.

Three bartenders for such a crowd was the bare minimum, anyway.

"*What can I get you guys?*" Cleo shouted over the song.

"*Two shots of Patron and a couple of beers!*" Deacon shouted back as he slid her a bill.

Cleo made an impressed face and I cringed. Both of them laughed at me. When I'd agreed that more drinks were needed, I didn't know that Deacon had planned to jumpstart our evening. However, due to the festivities currently underway, I felt it was my duty to go along with his plan.

When in Rome, and all that.

Within a minute, Cleo had placed two colorful plastic shot glasses in front of us, along with two Bud Lights with the caps popped off.

"*Sorry!*" she shouted. "*The beer selection is limited tonight to make things easy on everyone!*"

Deacon and I waved her off, indicating that we understood, and she gave us a wink before moving on to the next impatient drinker waiting their turn. Deacon and I grabbed our shot glasses, tapped them, and after a deep breath, kicked them back. Deacon handled his shot better than I did, but I'd never been a big shot taker. I like my liquor sipped or watered down with a mixer.

Grabbing our beers, we moved away from the bar, sipping at them as we made our way to the dancing area on the restaurant side. Though it was probably imprudent, I let Deacon grab my waist as he led me to the center of the floor. We danced and sipped beers with everyone else, laughing and smiling, acting foolish to the sounds of modern-day queer pop. I forgot all about the fact that the current situation with Deacon was fleeting. Pushing away thoughts of how he'd feel being rejected after our weekend together, I resolved to simply have fun.

Deacon and I danced, taking turns periodically to go to the bar for another round of beers. As the night wore on, I took plenty of opportunities in my inebriated state to check out the out-of-towners. Tourists of all shapes and sizes—almost all of them pleasing—provided eye candy on the temporary dancefloor in my mother's restaurant. Many of the men shirtless, or severely underdressed, definitely stood out from the locals who had come to the rave to simply have a fun Saturday night.

While the dancing was fun, the eye candy was sweet, and the beers were keeping both Deacon and I in high spirits, by midnight, it became clear that the crowd was shifting. Harper's was turning into the type of crowd that I typically avoided. I'm not one for losing teeth or waking up with bruises—nor do I enjoy spending nights in a drunk tank. Deacon seemed to pick up on the shifting vibe of the place as well. Eventually, the locals' drunken frustrations with the tourists were going to heat up. Hopefully, we were wrong, but I didn't want to stick around to find out.

"Should we get out of here while the getting is good?" Deacon screamed into my ear over the music.

Sweaty and tired, I laughed and gave him a simple nod. He grabbed my hand with a grin and led me from the dancefloor. At the corner by the door, we tossed our empty bottles in one of the giant trash cans set up for the evening. Deacon was about to lead me out the front door when it occurred to me that I hadn't said anything to Deb all night. In fact, I hadn't even seen her. If I left the Rainbow Rave without talking to her—an event she'd sponsored and hosted at her place of business for the Pride Weekend I'd organized—she'd kill me. And rightfully so.

"Wait!" I tugged at Deacon's hand at the door.

"What is it?" he asked, concern etching his face.

"I gotta at least say 'hi' and 'bye' to Deb," I said. "She did all this for Pride Weekend for me, I can't just leave."

Deacon gave me a warm smile.

"I'll be out by the car," he said. "Take all the time you need."

"Thanks!" I shouted over the music as I pushed my way back through the crowd.

Winding my way back through the crowd in my inebriated fashion, I found that all of the hot, shirtless guys bumping against me didn't bother me at all. Unlike my local brethren, I was finding the tourists an absolute delight. At least for that particular evening. I exchanged more than a few flirtatious smiles with the men I had to squeeze by on my way to find Deb. However, after several minutes of searching and still not finding her, I headed to the bar once again.

It took a while to force my way to the front of the line. Though I wouldn't have advised anyone in the bar to drink more than they already had, it certainly hadn't occurred to them. Everyone was getting as drunk as possible in order to enjoy the rest of the evening at Harper's before the bar closed—or they were kicked out. At the front of the line a few minutes later, I had to shout over the music again to get Cleo's attention.

"*Have you seen Deb?*" I asked loudly.

Cleo, leaning over the bar, replied with a response she practically had to scream.

"*I think she went out back for a smoke!*"

Rolling my eyes and laughing, I gave Cleo a nod I hoped she interpreted as a thanks.

Instead of trying to make my way through the restaurant and through the crowd to the backdoor, I fought my way to the front door. Surprised by the influx of people still trying to get inside, I managed to get outside, grateful for the fresh nighttime air. The stuffiness and heat of the interior of Harper's hadn't been obvious all evening. Now, standing in the cool nighttime air, I realized that I was basically a puddle of sweat in clothing. My curls were plastered to my head, and I had to look as though I'd just exited a sauna.

Breathing deeply to clear my lungs of the interior of Harper's, I looked across the parking lot and waved, getting Deacon's attention. He was seated on the hood of his car, enjoying the coolness of the night compared to the restaurant. He waved back when I gestured that I was stepping around the side of the building. Whether or not he understood didn't matter. He knew that I hadn't forgotten about him and would return promptly.

As I made my way around the side of the building to the dumpsters—where Deb always took her smoke breaks when the place was full—the sounds of the party became muffled. I could still hear the "thump-a thump-a" of the music inside, and the sound of voices filtered through the walls, but the party seemed to fade into the background. Relieved to be free of the sounds, the colors, lights, and smells, I tipped my head back to breathe in the fresh air.

Halfway along the side of the building, different sounds cut through those of the muffled party. Something like a rustling, or something banging around, reached my ears. When the sounds of cursing and muffled screams joined in, I started to run, my heart suddenly thundering in my chest. A howl of a scream, that sounded like a man, tore through the night as I reached the edge of the building. When I rounded the corner, someone was dashing off towards Wilford Woods. I was fairly certain they were wearing a black hoodie.

With my heart threatening to come out of my chest, my head whipped around, looking for Deb. When I turned towards the dumpsters, I found her, slumped on the ground like a rag doll. Rushing over, I skidded to a stop and knelt next to her. In the two seconds it took me to reach her, she was already sitting up, cursing and muttering. Her jeans were ripped at the thigh and her hair was a mess, but I didn't see any blood gushing out of any knife wounds.

"Mom!" I gasped as I knelt next to her, helping her to sit up. "Are you okay?"

"Sonof—" she began, grumbling as she rose from the ground.

"Are you hurt?" I demanded, cutting her off.

Deb didn't have time to answer. Suddenly, Deacon was coming around the corner of the building, out of breath. Looking up at him, I knew I had to look as panicked as I had the previous night when he was nearly stabbed.

"Get Jeremy, Deacon!" I commanded.

Without a word he took off back in the direction he'd come. I glanced over my shoulder towards Wilford Woods, but my mom's attacker had disappeared.

"Deb," I said, trying to sound calmer, "are you okay? Did he hurt you?"

"I'm fine," she grumbled, rubbing her hands on the thighs of her jeans. "He was trying to choke me out. Can you believe that?"

I stared at her.

"Put my cigarette out on his neck," Deb cackled roughly, then coughed into the crook of her elbow several times. "Wasted a good cigarette, but it was worth it."

I couldn't help but smile, knowing that Deb was okay— and that she'd managed to hurt the man who had tried to harm her. My mind began racing with thoughts about why anyone would want to attack my mother. She was a loudmouth—it runs in the family—and she could be abrasive, but she had no real enemies. Unless my father had come back to town, but I knew for a fact he was still in prison. The reason for her attack was obvious.

The murderer wasn't done killing.

Of course, Deb hadn't been stabbed. The guy hadn't even tried to stab her. He'd choked her. Killers changing up their M.O. is fairly rare. However, I'd seen him dashing off into the woods. It was the same guy. I was certain. Even though I still had only caught his height and the black hoodie, I *knew* the same guy who had tried to attack Deacon had attacked Deb. Unfortunately, I didn't have long to think about it. By the time I'd gotten Deb to her feet—and she was lighting another cigarette—Deacon had returned.

"I can't find Jeremy," Deacon said, out of breath as he rounded the building once more. "He's gone."

Frowning, I said the one thing I didn't want to say.

"Get Marv, then," I replied. "We need to—"

"Hell, no!" Deb barked as she blew out smoke. "Don't you bring that old coot back here, Deacon."

"We have to tell the police what happened, Deb," I said. "You were just attacked. Nearly killed."

Deacon nodded furiously at her, backing me up.

"I'd rather be killed than tell that man anything," Deb said, and it was obvious her word was final.

I shot Deacon a desperate look, but he gave me a commiserating frown and shrugged. We couldn't force Deb to be a victim if she didn't want to be. Upset and more than a little worried, I looked off towards Wilford Woods.

Why had the suspect attacked Deb?

She wasn't a gay man.

Her attack completely obliterated the theories I'd shared with Sawyer earlier in the day.

When I looked back over at Deb, she was smoking a fresh cigarette as though all was right with the world. She was fussing and picking at the rip in her jeans, but otherwise, seemed unbothered. Deacon was standing by helplessly, unable to fix anything, looking to me for guidance. I had none to give. All I could do was let my eyes dart from my mother to the darkness of the woods beyond Harper's, wondering what was going on in our little town.

The murderer had attacked Deb—which didn't make sense at all. He'd killed two gay men who were out-of-towners. He'd attacked Deacon. Now Deb. Two tourists. Two townies. Three gay men, one straight woman. It didn't make any kind of sense. Nothing was lining up in my head.

One thing was for certain. Even if Jeremy had still been present at Harper's, I'm not certain he would have talked to me about it. With the strain in our relationship, he probably would have taken Deb's story down and done his best to use the information to solve the cases. However, I would have been iced out from discussing theories.

None of us would talk to Marv, so he was no help, either.

And the worst thing of all—our murderer seemed to be getting braver.

Chapter Twenty

"It's our hope that this inaugural Pride Weekend will be the beginning of a community-building tradition here in Head Rock Harbor." Marv was bloviating at the podium set up on the dais in the police department parking lot as Linda Wagner nodded vehemently at his side. *"A new tradition for a progressive era. A time for our community to celebrate inclusivity, positivity, and acceptance. Above all things— tolerance. With this first annual Pride Weekend—"*

Glancing around, I could see that the locals and tourists alike were eating up Marv's speech. Of course, there were a few townies, such as myself, who weren't completely sold. Those who were the most jaded of us exchanged sly grins and winks, then went back to standing in the blistering summer sun, listening to the chief prattle on endlessly. All I could do was pray for the end of Marv's speech to come before we all melted in the heat.

Marv loving the sound of his own voice was a fairly new thing. In the past, I'd known him to be a loquacious man, but only if you engaged him. He was never one to carry on, talking about things that meant nearly nothing, ad nauseam, until a person dreamed of choking him out. This new version of Marv—the version that allowed Linda Wagner to manipulate him into disliking me—was not my favorite version.

Keeping us in the sun to listen to him listen to his own voice was his worst offense, however.

I'd nearly skipped the Tolerance Conference on Sunday at three o'clock for a few reasons. One, I had a book signing to prepare for at the bookstore, which was to take place at seven. Two, I knew that it was going to be a scorcher of a day. Finally, and this was the best reason I had, I was still rattled from the night before and more than a little hungover when I woke up Sunday.

The experience of having my mother attacked outside of her restaurant had my nerves on edge. Having the remnants of alcohol working its way out of my body didn't help. When I'd woken up in the morning—*okay, late morning*—I'd immediately gone to the bathroom. After taking care of some business produced by the hangover, I'd jumped in the shower, using as little hot water as possible. Hoping to shock the hangover away, I'd washed in nearly freezing water.

Though food sounded disgusting, I forced myself to sit at the kitchen table in my comfy robe and eat some cereal. I accompanied the bland breakfast with a mug of coffee and a giant cup of water. One way or the other, I was going to get myself back to normal—or as close to something resembling it as I could—before the book signing later in the evening.

When Deacon texted me around lunchtime, thanking me for a wonderful night—save Deb's attack—I was still in my robe. Dealing with my hangover was worsened by the reminder that I had a bomb to drop on Deacon at some point. I pushed that thought from my head immediately. One crisis at a time—especially when others could wait. My hangover was the one thing I desperately needed to deal with before all others.

By the time I had to head out for the Tolerance Conference, I'd managed to dress smartly, get my curls under control, and not look like the living dead. As one of the last to arrive, I fortunately got to stand near the back of the parking lot, where getting away unnoticed quickly would be easiest. As expected, I found Mayor Linda Wagner up on the dais, along with Marv and Officer Ashley Riley. The five City Council members were seated on folding chairs at the back, overlooking the entire affair.

That had been an hour ago. Sweat was starting to roll down between my shoulder blades, drip through the small of my back, and into lower places. If Marv carried on much longer, I'd have a severe case of butt gravy. I worried that he was going to carry on until the BBQ on the square started at five o'clock.

How long can one talk about tolerance? I thought to myself as I reached up to wipe beads of sweat from my brow. *No one here is going to want to tolerate anything if this goes on much longer.*

"He sure can talk, can't he?" I stared at the sound to my right.

When I turned to see who had spoken quietly to me, I found Ainsley Bucksworth. Marv's daughter was standing next to me, staring through the crowd up at her father. Dressed in mid-thigh length shorts, a sensible, flowy top, and her hair up in a bun, Ainsley was dressed for summer.

Though she looked put out and dewy from the heat, she still had a smile for her father up on the dais. Not wanting to say anything rude about her father directly to her, I gave her a smile.

"It's okay," Ainsley leaned in to chuckle. "I know he should shut up and end things."

I couldn't help but join in with her muffled laughter.

"He's just putting on a show," Ainsley said, as if making an excuse for her father.

She knew that everyone in the crowd was growing tired of his speech.

"A show for whom?" I found myself asking her. "We're all ready for intermission."

She grinned wickedly at me, appreciating the joke.

"For the council," she whispered back. "He wants them to see he's still a good chief, can bring the community together, and that everyone loves him enough to stand out in the heat for hours."

Frowning, I stared at her for a moment. Since when did Marv try to impress the City Council members?

"Why?" I asked the obvious question.

She rolled her eyes, blowing out an annoyed breath.

"They've been talking about replacing him," she said. "And they aren't so sweet on Linda lately, either. Next election, I bet they all endorse anyone who runs against her—even if it's Mavis Attberry."

I couldn't help but smile at that, even though my brow stayed furrowed.

"All of these...*killings*...the bad press...people are getting fed up with dad," Ainsley said, shaking her head softly. "And let's face it, he's had his time. I've been telling him to retire for years. Maybe he should get out while the getting's good, you know?"

Her bun wobbled on her delicate head as she spoke. Fanning her face as she stared directly ahead, but kept talking to me, I could see she was having trouble with the heat as well.

"Pass the torch," Ainsley continued. "Let one of the younger guys step up. He's up there talking about progress, well…let's move forward. He can spend the last third of his life fishing on city pension, and the younger guys can handle all the stress and worry."

"Jeremy?" A thought occurred to me and came out of my mouth before I could stop it.

Ainsley nodded slowly.

"I imagine that's who the council has in mind to replace him," Ainsley said. "Even if Linda doesn't like it. They'll fight her tooth and nail. And they'll win. Because she won't fight too hard, hoping that'll win her some points and keep them from coming out against her come election time."

Staring at the side of Ainsley's head as she fanned herself for a while, it suddenly dawned on me why Jeremy had been the way he'd been for a while. If things were getting hairy, politically, down at the police department and the mayor's office, it was no wonder he was playing things close to his vest. It explained why he was leaning towards Marv's side of the fence currently.

If your boss is close to being pushed out of his job, and you stand to be promoted into his role, it's best to walk a tightrope until whatever happens…happens. If the mayor and your boss are doing everything they can to hold onto the power they have, you don't want to upset them, either.

Suddenly, I found myself feeling pity for Jeremy. Obviously, his life behind the scenes was not looking so great. It would also explain why he was drinking and pouring his heart out to Deb.

But he'd said he hadn't been talking to Deb.

"I suppose that's why Marv is making his presence known more?" I asked quietly. "He wants to ingratiate himself with the townsfolk?"

Ainsley shrugged. "Maybe. He won't listen to me. He's going to do everything he can to keep his job—even if retiring would be better for him."

We both shared a "parents are ridiculous" grin.

As I started to speak, the sound of a car pulling up alongside the police department caught my attention. When I turned to look, I saw one of the police cruisers parking at the side of the building and Jeremy sliding out of the driver's seat. Ignoring the crowd, he headed up to the dais and soon was standing with Officer Riley behind Marv. The interruption did nothing to stop Marv.

"Is that why your dad has everyone using cruisers?" I asked Ainsley, staring at Jeremy, who hadn't spotted me at the back of the crowd. "To make everything more official and professional?"

"Jeremy's car's in the shop," Ainsley said. "Dad hasn't said anything about everyone having to use cruisers."

"Oh," I said.

Another thing Jeremy hadn't shared with me due to the strain in our relationship.

"Yeah. Wheel or axel problem or something since the middle of the week," Ainsley said. "I don't know. Dad was complaining about Ashley and Jeremy having to double up or use his cruiser from time to time due to Jeremy's car being out of commission. You know the council won't approve more city vehicles right now. Especially after spending money on Pride Weekend."

The wheels in my head were turning, but they weren't going anywhere. Things that had been said over the last week—random, at the time meaningless things—were swirling around. But two and two didn't come out to equal four. It was simply an equation presented in my head, waiting for me to find the solution and prove its existence had meaning.

Tired of the heat and the droning of Marv's voice, I turned to Ainsley and gave her a smile.

"I'm going to slip out while I can," I said conspiratorially, drawing a sly grin from her. "I have to make sure the shop's ready for the book signing tonight."

"Oh!" She gasped with delight. "I have a ticket! I'll be there with bells on."

"We'll have to talk then," I said quietly. "I've been meaning to ask you about chairs for the new coffee bar."

"Can't wait," she replied.

Smiling, I gave her a nod, and I slipped away from the crowd, heading on foot back to Head Rock Harbor Books. The equation my mind had created in my head kept pulling at my attention, but no matter how much I tried to solve it, it simply sat there, mocking me.

Chapter Twenty-One

Having never hosted a book signing at the shop before, I humbly thought that I'd done a great job for my first. As I watched Taylor C. Tomlin laugh haughtily with a group of readers crowded around him by the coffee bar in the shop, nothing could ruin my mood. The trays of canapes I'd set out had been a hit. The wine, water, and soft drinks I'd made available for attendees were thoroughly enjoyed. All fifty ticketed guests had arrived on time and stood for the full thirty-minute reading Taylor had provided. No one even complained about the lack of seating. Most of all, Deacon and I, as we had hopped up to sit on the check-out counter for the reading.

Attendees had been respectful of the rope I'd tied across the stairs and hadn't tried to venture out of bounds upstairs. The downstairs bathroom hadn't been destroyed and no one had snuck out with free rolls of toilet paper, as far as I could tell. No one had tried to sneak into the storage room or walk off with free merchandise. In fact, the entire stock I'd ordered of Taylor's book had been sold out, and special orders had to be made for those who had missed their chance.

Though still not someone I personally enjoyed, I was pleased with Taylor sitting down and signing every single book that was presented to him. Behind the scenes, he might have been a lot to deal with, but to his readers, he was an angel. He made the bookstore—and me—look good. I would forever be indebted to the man, even if I'd never accept a dinner invitation from him.

The funniest part of the entire evening was how Rattlesnatches stalked the top of the bookcases, glaring down at the store full of strangers. Having his evening time invaded by unknowns was obviously not on his list of favorite things. Trying to get him off the bookcases and carry him upstairs to lock him away would have caused too much of a scene, so I let him be. Halfway through the event, after Taylor had finished reading, and the books were actually being signed, my furry buddy calmed down considerably. He even hopped down to go lay in the front window.

Once Rattlesnatches realized that the ticketholders for the event were good for head scratches and praise, he seemed to think book signings were the best thing ever. The worst part of the evening, however, was the affection Deacon bestowed upon me. Taking every chance he could to hold my hand, lace an arm around my waist, and smile moonily up at me had my stomach twisting tightly in knots. I'd gotten over my hangover, so it wasn't our Saturday night still wreaking havoc on my body. I knew we were closing in on what had to be done.

I simply wasn't looking forward to letting him down.

The book signing was such a success, and everyone was having so much fun, that things were still going strong as the time for the Rainbow Fireworks was fast approaching. And no one was indicating that they were going to leave to attend. Seeing that the night was supposed to be coming to an end and everyone else was supposed to be moving on to another event, I began winding my way through the crowd a quarter 'til nine. Reminding everyone that the fireworks would be starting soon, it didn't take long to get most of the shop cleared of guests. Deacon chipped in, mirroring my actions to help me get people out the door.

Finally, I approached Taylor and the throng of guests who were crowded around him, listening to him regale them with some, apparently, engaging tale.

"Black sports car—something sporty anyway," Taylor was saying as I approached. "Nearly ran me down! Your town is just lovely, don't get me wrong, but some people simply can't drive."

The people around him laughed, several admitting he wasn't wrong.

"It was insane!" Taylor continued, chuckling jovially, sipping a glass of wine. "Right at the far end of Harbor Street here on Tuesday. Nearly ran me down, sped down the street when I leaped out of the way, then even hit the corner curb at the end of the street when it turned to speed away. I felt like I was in a cop show!"

Everyone laughed as I approached, getting their attention.

"I hate to break up the party," I said cheerfully. "You've been so great, Taylor. Really."

The people around us made their agreement clear.

214

"But the Rainbow Fireworks display is starting soon," I said over their voices. "You all don't want to miss that. Rexie and Tommy told me it's going to be absolutely spectacular."

Tommy and Rexie had said it would be "nice" with the budget they had, but I figured playing things up a bit would get people out of the shop quicker. I had to remind everyone to leave their glass of wine on the coffee bar, as drinking on a public street in Head Rock Harbor wasn't necessarily legal. Over some grumbles of annoyance, I managed to get everyone legal and out of the shop, Taylor being the last out the door.

When I turned from the closed door, I found Deacon standing by the check-out counter, smiling oddly at me.

"What?" I chuckled and leaned back against the door.

"Can I say something weird?" he asked softly.

"Sure," I said. "Better than anyone I know."

He grinned.

"Jeremy has a black sports car—*something sporty anyway*," Deacon said, frowning.

"You heard Taylor?"

"Yeah," Deacon said. "I did. And Jeremy has a car that matches that description."

"So do a million other dudes his age who don't know how to grow up," I said, laughing as I walked over to join him at the counter. "But his is in the shop. He couldn't have tried to run Taylor over."

Deacon stared at me for a moment. "Since when?"

"Since when what?"

"When did he put it in the shop?"

"Uh, middle of the week?" I shrugged. "That's what Ainsley said today."

"For what reason?" Deacon crossed his arms over his chest.

"Wheel or axel issue?" I shrugged again. "Jeremy isn't exactly talking to me lately. Or I would ask him myself. Maybe. It's not really my business."

Deacon's brow rose.

"What?" I laughed.

"Taylor nearly gets run over by a black sports car on Tuesday—a black sports car that hits the curb on its way speeding off," Deacon said. "And then Jeremy ends up putting his car in the shop in the middle of the week to fix a tire or axel issue?"

I waved him off.

"Stop being ridiculous," I said. "Jeremy didn't try to run Taylor down. If he'd met him, I'd tend to agree with you. However, Jeremy doesn't even know Taylor enough to want him dead. Or even hurt. He'd have no reason to do that."

"Hm." Deacon made a humming noise.

"What's that supposed to mean?" I frowned.

Deacon stared at me for a moment, then his frown disappeared and he was smiling again.

"I'm sorry," he said. "It was stupid. You're right. A million guys own that type of car. "I shouldn't have even brought it up."

"No worries," I said, my own frown melting away. "I get it."

Deacon sidled up to me at the check-out counter and batted his eyes at me with a smile.

"So," he said, "should we go see the fireworks together?"

I shrugged.

"Or do you…wanna…do something else?" he asked softly.

It would have taken a complete idiot to not miss the implication in Deacon's voice. Staring down into his eyes, I knew the time had come to break his heart. Now that I knew he thought we'd progressed to *that* stage in our dating, I couldn't let things go any further.

"How about a walk?" I asked suddenly, pushing away from the counter.

Deacon, smiling quizzically, followed my lead. I made sure I had my wallet and keys, and we exited the shop, the bell jangling overhead as we left. I turned off the lights and locked the door behind us. When I got back to the shop, I'd clean up the leftover trays of food and drinks, but dealing with Deacon was more important.

As we walked, heading west on Harbor Street and away from the fireworks display in the harbor, Deacon grabbed my hand and laced his fingers through mine. We were on the next block before the first firework whistled through the air and burst into the sky above. The street ahead of us flashed red, white, blue, and green as we walked. As the fireworks continued behind us, the cheers of the crowd in the distance reached our ears as I led Deacon down the street.

We were nearly to his apartment before Deacon said something.

"Are we going to my place?" he asked softly, hopefully.

"We are," I said.

"Okay," he said, happily. "Don't mind the mess. I haven't decluttered in a few—"

"I'm not taking you to your place to sleep with you Deacon," I said as we approached the front door of his apartment building.

Turning to me as he used his fob to open the lobby door for us, I gave him a difficult smile and stepped inside with him. Once we were out of the tepid nighttime air, I turned to face him. He already had one of my hands, so I reached out and took his other, holding them both as I looked him in the eyes. When I opened my mouth to speak, he stopped me.

"Jeremy," he said simply.

I was going to deny it, but I would have been lying. Jeremy wasn't the only reason that I was going to reject Deacon. It wasn't the only reason that Deacon and I wouldn't work, but he was part of it. To deny it was to lie.

"Jeremy," I said back with a nod.

Deacon slid his hands from mine and he smiled softly, though I could see the hurt in his face.

"Okay," he said. "I mean, that really hurts, but thank you for being honest. Early. Not waiting until it would have hurt a lot more."

"I'm sorry," I said to Deacon. "I really am. I actually really like you. You're a lot of fun. But you're a friend kind of fun. Not a boyfriend kind of fun."

He sighed.

"I get that," he said finally. "And, don't take this personally, but I really need to go upstairs now."

I nodded slowly. "Okay. Talk soon?"

"Give me a few days, but…yeah. Soonish," Deacon said as he turned to leave. At the last moment, he seemed to have a thought, then turned back to me. "But can I say something else about Jeremy really quickly?"

"Sure," I said. "I owe you that much."

"The first victim?" Deacon said, surprising me. "Looked like me. I was also attacked at the Rainbow Lights. Your mom was attacked. It seems like the victims have a connection to you. One who has…*had*…a romantic interest in you. And there's the car thing. Think about that."

"The second guy has no connection to me at all," I said. "But I appreciate you trying to help figure things out."

I'd made myself clear. I wasn't going to listen to the implication in Deacon's words. Seeing the resolve in my face, Deacon simply nodded, turned, and headed off toward the stairs at a brisk pace. A moment later, he'd slipped into the stairwell and was gone. I stood there, watching after him for a moment, wishing I hadn't had to hurt him.

When I turned to exit the lobby, his words were pounding in my head suddenly. The first victim looked like Deacon. The attack came after Jeremy saw me at Harper's with him on a date. The second victim…*looked like Taylor C. Tomlin.* I'd told Jeremy that I thought Taylor was attractive. A second attack happened to Deacon during our second date, though it failed. And then the murderer tried to kill Deb. A person who knew Jeremy was jealous and upset about my romantic situation with Deacon.

One thing I knew about jealousy, it was a great motive.

Especially for murder.

Murders.

The equation in my head started to make a lot of sense, especially with all of the new information I'd gathered over the weekend. Before I could stop myself, I was racing across the lobby to the elevator. I leapt inside when it arrived in the lobby and hit the button for the third floor. Less than a minute later, I was knocking on the door to 3E, hoping Ms. Annetta Bowles was not the type to enjoy fireworks.

It took a few minutes, but finally, the sound of her approaching the door and disengaging the lock reached my ears. When she pulled the door back, the look of surprise and delight on her face was apparent.

"It's you again!" she exclaimed. "Jackson? Jackson Harper!"

"That's me," I said hurriedly.

"Well, what brings you—"

"Are you sure no one else lives here?" I asked her.

"Well," she actually thought about it, "no, baby. It's just me. Has been the whole time I've lived here."

My heart sank, but I refused to give up.

"Can you think of anyone who maybe lives in one of the other apartments on this floor," I asked quickly, "who's a little taller than me. A guy? Wears black hoodies a lot? Anything like that?"

I knew my description of the suspect was insane. Millions of people across the world would fit the description. However, Annetta Bowles, I *knew*, was the key to figuring everything out. When she finally answered after thinking about it for a while, my heart sank.

"No, hun," she said, shaking her head. "I'm sorry. No one I can think of."

With a great sigh, I did my best to smile at her.

"Well," I said, "thanks anyway. Sorry for, uh, bothering you again."

I turned and started to walk back down the hall to the elevators.

"Have a good night," I said over my shoulder with a wave.

"You too!" she replied cheerfully. "I'll asked my nephew next time he's over if he's seen anyone like that and I'll call you at the bookstore if he has. He was here yesterday, and earlier today, I wish I'd thought to task him."

Stopping in my tracks, my heart skipped a beat. I turned to look down the hallway at Ms. Bowles.

"Who," I asked slowly, "is your nephew?"

I wanted to be shocked at the name she gave me.

But I wasn't.

Deacon was right.

Jealousy was a hell of a motive.

Chapter Twenty-Two

Seated at the kitchen table up in my apartment, I was tapping my fingers nervously on the wooden top, my mind surprisingly calm. My laptop was to the side of the table, open, but untouched. I had to focus on other things right now. My body was a ball of jitters and knots, but my mind was clear. The equation that had formulated in my brain had found the solution. I'd proven the reason for its existence. I hadn't been having my niggling little feelings and random thoughts for no reason. There really was something to all of the things that had been staring me in the face all week long and all through Pride Weekend.

Deacon made me realize that I'd been blind to the clues right in front of my face.

Since talking to Annetta Bowles and leaving Deacon's apartment, I'd gone over everything in my head at least three times. The victims, the evidence, sightings of the suspect, everything that was being kept from me, and everything that was right in front of my face. No matter how I painted the canvas, it still made the same picture.

One thing my detective and true murder shows never taught me was how to feel when the guilty party was someone you cared about. Someone from your own community. Someone you had considered a friend for years. What does one do when you realize that you are going to have to help put away someone you know and care about? Because no matter what, the right thing was what I was going to do.

I knew who had killed the two tourists and had attacked Deacon and my mother. Preparing myself mentally for that was all I could do as I sat in the kitchen. Even Rattlesnatches wasn't much of a comfort. I'd locked him away in the upstairs storage room with his litter box, food, and water. Having him out of the way for a few hours was integral. I was inviting danger into my home, and making sure Rattlesnatches wasn't accidentally collateral damage was important to me.

There was no reason both of us had to put ourselves in harm's way.

When I heard the footsteps downstairs, coming from the backdoor, through the store, and to the stairs, I sat up in my chair. I was sitting at the table on the side that faced the open door to the apartment. Making sure I had eyes on whoever came through the door was not only smart, it was integral to everything.

As the footsteps sounded up the staircase and along the balcony to the apartment, I made sure I looked relaxed and nonconfrontational. I wanted to appear as though this was the same as any other late night at my apartment. Nothing was out of the ordinary. Just Jackson Harper, enjoying a quiet night of contemplation after a long Pride Weekend, thinking about getting ready for bed. Or maybe considering which movie to watch before nodding off.

The sound of footsteps reached the door, and I looked up.

"Hey," Jeremy said as he came out of the shadows and into the doorway.

"Hey back," I replied as I discreetly unlocked my phone and shot off a text.

Smiling oddly, he stepped into the apartment, his phone in his hand.

"What's going on, Jacks?" he asked. "I got your text and—"

"Sit down," I said. "Would you? Please?"

Frowning deeply so that the middle of his forehead was one big crease, Jeremy shuffled over to the kitchen table. He sat down across from me and set his phone on the table. Chewing at my lip, I considered how I should start laying things out for him. Jeremy had always been my best friend. Even though we hadn't been getting along lately, that didn't change anything. Having hard conversations with your best friend should be easier than they are with anyone else.

"You've been jealous," I said simply.

Jeremy started to roll his eyes, realized there was no one else around, and, instead, grew rosy cheeked. Instead of denying what I'd said, he folded his hands atop the table and stared down at them. He didn't respond to what I'd said, but he didn't deny it.

"Me hanging out with Sawyer," I began, "who's just a friend, by the way. And then me going on several dates with Deacon."

He kept his eyes on his hands as his fingers fiddled with each other.

"I get it," I said. "In the past, though I didn't recognize the feelings at the time, I was jealous every time I saw you with some guy."

Jeremy glanced up at me, then his eyes were back on his hands.

"You've lived your life a certain way, and I've lived mine a certain way," I said. "Absolutely no judgment for how you've run your romantic life, Germ. That's not what I'm about to say is about. Okay?"

He was quiet for a long moment, then nodded.

"But I learned to get over you," I said. "The whole town's-a-talkin'. Jeremy Morris and Jackson Harper have been so close for so long. Best friends. Both gay. When are they finally going to give up the ghost and admit they should be dating?"

A small smile quirked at the corner of his mouth, but he didn't look up.

"But I taught myself to not look at you that way," I said. "Because you chose to…do what you want to do. You never indicated to me that you had any romantic interest in me. I'm going to be completely honest with you here, okay?"

Jeremy looked up, nodded, then his eyes were on his hands again.

"Yeah," I couldn't help but chuckle, "I was absolutely over the moon for you all through high school. Hottest guy in the whole world. When I was away at college? I couldn't wait to come home on breaks. Not to see Mom or Belinda. I wanted to catch up with you."

Jeremy was smiling even though he wasn't looking at me.

"And you kept dating other guys," I said. "Rubbing my face in it. Not caring at all what it was doing to me. Oblivious. But…then again…I never told you how I felt."

He nodded.

"And, I thought you were rubbing all your conquests in my face. Maybe you were," I said, shrugging. "Because you didn't have the nerve to tell me how you felt, either."

He didn't respond, but his nervous finger movements increased.

"But you probably weren't too worried about it." I continued. "I wasn't dating *anyone*. I was staying single and not even daring to mingle. *Eventually he'll give me some indication I should ask him out*, you probably were thinking."

Jeremy's cheeks grew rosier.

"But I never did," I said, sighing. "Because I'm an idiot jerk, I guess. So, you finally bit the bullet and kissed me. Laid your cards out on the table. And I rejected you. Do you know why?"

Jeremy looked up at me, suddenly interested.

"Because I wasn't special," I said. "You didn't take me out to Harper's. Or The Dock. Or play a round a pool and dance with me at Harper's. You wanted me to come right over to your place and…well, you know. You gave me less consideration than the strange men you hooked up with after hanging out at Harper's."

My best friend hung his head and his fingers stopped moving. Obviously, he hadn't considered how his indecent proposal had come off at the time.

"I was both dying inside from excitement that you finally took notice of me," I said, "and equally felt like crap. Even if I wasn't going to be a simple notch on your bedpost, I wasn't special enough to even be asked out for a drink. But a one-night stand had the chance to be wooed by you. Do you see what I'm saying?"

Jeremy nodded. He looked up, catching my eyes for a moment, then nodded more firmly, and went back to looking at his hands.

"Sorry, Jacks," Jeremy said. "All I was thinking at the time was...*lock it down, Morris. You have the nerve now. In this moment. Don't lose it.* I didn't want to take time to convince myself to keep my thoughts to myself again."

I shrugged. "You didn't mean to upset me. I'm not mad. Not anymore. And, I'm honestly more upset with myself because I carry half the blame. Not saying how I felt to you either left the entire burden on you—and I wanted you to be perfect. It wasn't fair."

Jeremy gave me a grateful smile, and for once, didn't look down at his hands.

He sighed and picked up his phone, looking at the screen.

"Is that what the text was about?" Jeremy said, reading from his phone. "*I need to talk to you. It's important. Come in the backdoor. I changed the code to 675543.*"

"Partially," I said. "I wanted to clear the air before anything else happened."

"To be clear," Jeremy said, "you're saying if I ask you out properly, treat you special, maybe you'll say 'yes'?"

I stared at him for a long moment.

"Well," I said, "we need to talk about the fact that you've been jealous for a moment longer. And what jealousy does to people. The things it makes them do."

Jeremy eyed me suspiciously, tensing in his seat.

"The first victim at the sandbar?" I began immediately. "Looked like Deacon. The second victim? Looked like Taylor C. Tomlin. I told you he was attractive. Deacon was attacked during our date at the Rainbow Lights. Then, Deb was attacked at the Rainbow Rave after I told you she had implied you'd been pouring your heart out to her about me."

Frowning more deeply, Jeremy was processing what I was saying to him.

"Jealousy is a big feeling," I said calmly. "It's a great motive. Especially for things like murder."

Jeremy's frown turned to a look of indignation. I glanced at his phone on the table to see the time. I took a deep breath as Jeremy pushed back from the table, rising to his feet.

"Is that what you think?" Jeremy stammered. "You think I'd do that? That I'm capable of those kinds of things? That I killed those people? That I attacked Deacon and Deb? That, maybe, I came here tonight when you asked so I could kill you, even?"

He was red in the face for a different reason now as he towered over me, glaring down at me angrily. Calmly, I stared up at him.

"No, Germ," I said quietly. "I think you're here tonight to make sure I don't get killed."

"What?" Jeremy stammered, his anger replaced with confusion.

I started to speak, but the bells over the door in the shop below jangled, followed by the silent cursing of the person entering.

Chapter Twenty-Three

"Hey, there," I said casually.

I was typing on my laptop when Officer Ashley Riley stepped out of the shadows of the balcony and into the doorway of my apartment. Pretending to be transfixed by whatever I was working on, I acted as if I wasn't watching him closely.

"You got my text I sent you a few minutes ago?" I asked, looking at the computer screen.

"I did," he said cautiously as he stepped further into the apartment.

"The text didn't tell you to come here," I said. "I told you I wanted to meet with you tomorrow for lunch at Munchies. About your involvement in the recent murders."

He took a few steps closer, but stopped several feet from the table.

"But here you are," I said, pushing my laptop from out of in front of me.

"What did you mean?" Ashley asked, stuffing his hands in his pockets casually. "My involvement? I have no idea what you're talking about."

Sighing, I tried not to focus on his hands in his pockets. Having them out in the open, clearly in sight, would have been best. However, I was not currently in a position to demand that he keep his hands where I could see them. Only one of us had an actual weapon.

"You did a really good job," I said. "Covering your tracks and motive."

Ashley stared at me.

"Jealousy," I said, nodding slowly. "It's a good motive. A lot of people are jealous. Makes a lot of people look guilty. Especially my best friend."

He said nothing, and his hands stayed in his pockets, so I continued.

"I heard Marv might be shown the door and a severance," I said, changing course. "That's going to shake things up a lot at the department, huh?"

Ashley frowned at me, confused by the sudden change in topic.

"I was talking to Ainsley at the Tolerance Conference?" I said, sitting back in my chair casually. "She said that the City Council is wanting to oust Marv. Linda might even go along with it, even though she's besties with Marv, in order to save her own career, come election time. We all know when it comes down to the nitty gritty, that woman isn't going to torpedo her political ambitions and give up control for someone like Marv."

Watching me closely, Ashley slid his hands from his pockets. Fortunately, they were empty. I kept my eyes on his.

"So," I said, "Marv will have to be replaced. I'm betting Jeremy is on every City Council member's mind at the moment. Don't you?"

Ashley glowered at me.

"He's a good cop. Good detective. Community loves him," I said. "He's a good choice. Wouldn't you agree?"

Again, more glowering from the officer standing in my apartment.

"You probably don't." I chuckled as though I was the dumbest person in the world. "I mean, why Jeremy? Why is that the logical choice for our next chief? Why not...*you*?"

Ashley backed up until he was against the kitchen counter and leaned against it, crossing his arms over his chest as he stared at me.

"Marv was on his way out," I said, draping an arm over the back of my chair casually as I spoke to Ashley. "It was only a matter of time. After Prescott Pemberton, Marshelle Martin, Carter Nelson and his family, how Mavis was treated...the fact that a normal, average citizen basically did all of his work for him. He had to depend on his one detective and a *bookstore owner* to figure out two murders and a suspicious death? People are getting tired of him and his laziness and incompetence. And when people find out he's kept two murders quiet to protect himself and the mayor? It'll be the nail in the coffin. I'll be surprised if Linda doesn't end up smelling like rotten garbage after all's said and done, right?"

He shrugged, so I continued.

"So," I said, "why not hurry the process along? Make him look even more incompetent? Of course, doing that only means he's out quicker and Jeremy is chief and your boss quicker, am I right?"

He said nothing, but he gave me the slightest of nods.

"I thought so," I said, nodding along. "So, what to do, what to do? The only thing that would give you a shot at being named chief—even if only interim—would be if Jeremy was out of the picture, too. Right?"

Ashley actually smiled, and reached up to scratch the back of his head as he looked down at his feet.

"You know," I began, "with Jeremy and I kind of on the outs lately, I should have known he'd be looking for someone else to talk to about his life. Someone to listen to his woes. Someone he sees almost every day. I bet he's poured his heart out to you a lot over the last month and a half, hasn't he?"

"A bit," Ashley finally said something. "Maybe a lot."

"And maybe you've been letting off steam having a few drinks at Harper's on your night's off? Talking to my mother about…things. Things that will make Jeremy look jealous of me. Insanely, *murderously* jealous. Things she'd pass along to me to make me suspicious. So, when I also solved this case, I'd point the finger at Jeremy."

The grin on Ashley's face grew.

"The only problem is," I said, "there's no world in which my mother—or I—would believe the murderous part. Insane? Sure. Jeremy's not always right in the head. But I'd never believe he killed anyone. Especially because he was jealous of me dating other guys."

The grin melted from Ashley's face.

"You killing the guy who looked like Deacon after you and Jeremy saw on us on a date at Harper's?" I asked. "That was smart. Attacking the guy behind my shop who looked like Taylor C. Tomlin after Jeremy probably complained about me finding him attractive? Super smart. Made both Jeremy and I look guilty if the right person examined the evidence. That is—after you nearly ran him over in Jeremy's car. You've been doing a lot of personal errands for your coworkers? Isn't that what Marv said in his speech the other night? Does that included gassing up their vehicles, taking them to get washed…and then taking them to the shop after you nearly destroy one of their axels hopping a curb? And I bet taking Jeremy's car to the shop was when you managed to make a key to my front door so you would be ready if you had to kill me, right? Did you also come into the shop the other day when y'all were investigating the murder in the alley, see the lug nut, and remove it to look like Jeremy was hiding evidence?"

The look of absolute hatred on Ashley's face had me concerned. I didn't know where his gun was—but it wasn't in sight.

"Attacking Deacon during the Rainbow Lights—then attacking Deb during the Rainbow Rave?" I nodded slowly. "Again, makes Jeremy look both jealous and as though he was trying to take Deb out since she knew he was jealous. But Deb's attack wasn't just about the jealousy angle, was it? You wanted to take her out so she couldn't tell anyone that *you* were the one who was planting seeds in her head and feeding her information about Jeremy, huh?"

Ashley was standing rigid now, glowering at me from his space by the cabinets.

"I bet if you lower your collar, we'll find a cigarette burn," I said casually.

Ashley, suddenly smirking, reached up to pull the collar of his shirt down slightly. An angry red circle decorated the side of his neck.

"So, a couple of people died due to jealousy," I said finally. "But not Jeremy's. Yours. I bet seeing Jeremy get all the accolades for his detective work over the last several months burned your butt. And having me, a normal, average citizen help him only made it worse. Seeing the possibility of him becoming police chief and your boss was the final straw. He had to go. Committing murders he couldn't solve and that would eventually be pinned on him...*feeding gossip anonymously to reporters in Dubuque*...you really had a plan laid out to swoop in for Marv's job."

"So what?" Ashley said. "I'll be a great police chief. Sometimes you have to kill a few people to get what you want. And you can't prove any of this."

"You might've made a great police chief," I said with a shrug. "But you made a mistake."

Ashley squinted at me.

"Your aunt Annetta?" I chuckled. "You never should have tried to attack Deacon at his apartment building. Maybe people could be convinced that Jeremy went to Deacon's place to try to throw him down the stairs—but you having been seen there numerous times, and your aunt living right next door to him? That's kind of sloppy, man."

Ashley was inching closer.

"She's a nice woman," I said. "Your aunt. She said she's going to check out the shop sometime soon. I promised to give her a senior discount."

"So what?" Ashley stammered as he approached the table, gripping the edge to glare down at me. "You can't prove anything. And when you're dead, you won't have the chance to try."

"Another mistake, Ashley," I said, my eyes flicking over to my laptop. "You're currently being beamed out on the shop's Instagram Live. And—"

I looked carefully at the screen.

"—forty-seven followers have joined us. Say 'hi' if you want because—"

Before I could react, Ashley was reaching around his back. Two things happened at once, I was frantically pushing back in my chair, hoping to get myself out of the line of fire, and a series of "pops" boomed through the apartment. I fell to the floor, all noise suddenly sounding as if it was being beamed to me through water. Shaking my head, I was on my hands and knees on the floor, my vision slightly blurry with panic and the sound of someone talking in gibberish seemed to fill the room. Time was slow. I was floating through water. Then time sped up, returned to normal. Everything started to return to normal. Somehow, I managed to push to my knees and look for Jeremy.

He was on the other side of the kitchen. I could see him through my view under the table. Jeremy was rolling Ashley onto his back, simultaneously kicking away the gun Ashley had tried to draw on me. Echoes and watery sounds continued in my ears for a moment as I did my shaky best to rise to my feet. Sirens. In the distance. Somewhere there was sirens.

Jeremy was saying something to Ashley as he cuffed him, then speaking into his walkie. It took a moment, but finally, my ears seemed to clear, and the room came back to me.

"—wearing a vest, but three shots," Jeremy was speaking calmly into the walkie. "He'll need medical attention. Is Marv on his way?"

"I hear sirens," I said simply as I shakily made my way to my feet.

Jeremy shot a look over at me, then cocked his head to listen. He nodded at me.

"I hear him," he said, then spoke into the walkie again. "Get that ambulance here now."

"Jeremy," I said simply, not knowing what else to say.

I was staring down at him as he kept his knee in the back of the very upset—and very pained—police officer who had just tried to kill me. Jeremy looked up at me, barely contained rage behind his comforting smile.

"No one takes three to the chest, even in a vest, and stays upright, Jacks," he said. "You're safe now. I promise. Sit down. Please sit down."

Suddenly, it dawned on me that I was swaying, my knees barely staying locked. I flopped into the nearest chair. Then, seeing my laptop still open, I slapped it shut.

"You have the right to remain silent—" Jeremy began as I sat there, willing myself to not be sick.

Jealousy is strong. Facing your mortality is stronger.

All I could do was sit there and stare. Even as the bells over the door below jangled and Marv was suddenly rushing into the apartment, I sat and stared. Everything he said and asked was a blur. When the paramedics showed up, I sat and stared. Once Ashley was taken away, it took Jeremy coming over to wrap his arms around me and pull me up from the chair for me to break my catatonic state.

"Come on," he said. "You're safe. I've got you. I won't let anything happen to you. Let's get you checked out, Jacks."

And I followed, my feet practically dragging along.

Chapter Twenty-Four

Stepping out into the blazing sun and the humidity of summer, I felt my curls immediately frizz and slump on my head. I reached up and ran frustrated, yet amused, fingers through them. For the rest of summer, I'd be fighting against the humidity of a river town and the war it waged on my curls. I'd been doing it for most of my life. Even if I wasn't happy about it, it was a way of life I'd become accustomed to enduring.

I pinched the front of my t-shirt and shook it a few times, letting air waft up and cool me slightly. Looking around, it didn't take long to find Jeremy. He was sitting on the corner bench outside the police department, staring down at his phone, smiling. Probably watching silly videos—or maybe one of his sports teams had scored a goal of some kind.

Stuffing my hands in my pockets and strolling down the street and away from the office, I felt a little better. When I approached the bench and Jeremy noticed me, then looked up, the smile that immediately overtook his face made all my worries melt away. He rose from the bench, locking his phone and sliding it into his pocket. Reaching out, he popped me softly under the chin with a light fist.

"How ya' holding up?" he asked.

"The shrink thinks I'll be okay," I said. "Some PTSD, the nightmares are normal, etcetera, etcetera, ad nauseam, on and on, so forth and so on. But he recommended a counselor he thinks will help me sort myself out fully."

Jeremy smiled.

"Surprisingly," I leaned in to give an exaggerated whisper, "the city is offering to pay for all of my counseling. Can you imagine?"

He laughed uproariously.

"So," I said when he quieted down, "I guess I'm going to see a counselor once a week for a bit. Just to make sure I wasn't driven insane by nearly getting shot in the face by a psychopath."

"I think that's a great idea," Jeremy said.

We stared at each other and smiled for a moment, then he cocked his head towards the north.

"Walk you back to the bookstore?" he asked.

"Sure," I said.

Jeremy stepped up, and wrapped an arm around my shoulders, then pulled me off the curb. We began walking north towards Harbor Street. Even with the heat, I felt better with his arm around my shoulders. Not simply because having my cop best friend's arm around me made me feel safe, but because something lower in me felt tingly at Jeremy's touch.

A week had passed since Officer Ashley Riley had tried to murder me in my apartment while nearly fifty of my patrons watched through the internet. After Jeremy had shot him, arrested him, and Ashley had been rushed to the hospital, it was decided that besides some bruising and a couple broken ribs, Ashley would make a full recovery. A few days later, he was unceremoniously shipped off to the county jail. Jeremy guaranteed me that he'd be there until his trial—and then he'd go to big-boy prison. There was no way he'd be found innocent of anything he'd done.

I wanted to believe Jeremy, but until I heard a verdict, I'd be nervous.

The entire town was in an uproar, calling for the heads of anyone who might have authority—except for Jeremy. He was hailed a hero. And that's because he was. When he'd immediately given me his trust and hidden in the bathroom of my apartment so we could see what Ashley would do, he was my hero. When he'd popped out to save me at just the right moment, he'd proven his prowess as a cop—and his excellent friendship skills.

I'd been checked out at the hospital that night as well. My catatonic fugue after the incident had Jeremy—and everyone else—worried about me. Although the doctor on duty had proclaimed me healthy and unharmed, I'd been kept overnight for observation. Jeremy never left my side. Even when he was pressured to leave to give statements or do paperwork, he told the City Council, the mayor, and Marv they'd have to wait until I was released the next morning. He laid in my hospital bed next to me, curled up on my side, holding me as I did my best to fitfully sleep.

In the morning, he and Marv had to sneak me out of the hospital. Which was when I finally got home to let Rattlesnatches out of the storage room. I thought he'd be mad at me, but he, surprisingly, seemed to understand. Due to the fact that I'd broadcast Ashley's confession and arrest online, reporters had gotten wind of the situation. Though they'd actually found Pride Weekend unworthy of their time, another series of murders in the sleepy town of Head Rock Harbor solved by the bookstore owner was a sensational story. I'd been avoiding them in the days since. A sign in the bookstore window made it clear they were not welcome on the premises.

I'd had to text Angel to let him know that the bookstore reopening, along with the new coffee bar, would be delayed by a week. I felt bad, knowing that Angel needed the job and the money, but things needed to cool off before I invited the public into my business and home once again. It being Monday, I hoped that opening the store the next day wouldn't set off some trauma response. But there was only one way to find out. And life had to get back to normal eventually.

With the pressure applied to Linda and Marv after the video of Ashley and me made the rounds, discovering the identity of the two murder victims quickly became a priority. In the end, Marv found out that both men had come to Head Rock Harbor with friends, but the friends had simply been drunk and disorderly all week, not really worrying when they disappeared. Everyone just assumed that each man had found someone to *have some fun with* during a Pride Weekend, and figured they'd pop back up after the event was over. Regardless, families were contacted. And those families were also calling for Linda's and Marv's heads.

"What did you find out?" I asked Jeremy as we walked. "From the council?"

"They're going to extend my paid leave by two weeks," he said casually.

"They can't do that!" I demanded, stopping and turning to look at him.

His arm fell from my shoulders and he smiled down at me.

"I asked them to," Jeremy said. "I want to watch after you for a bit. And I need the break."

"Oh," I said.

"The leave was only a formality anyway," Jeremy brushed it off. "I shot an officer. They had to put me on paid administrative leave while everything is investigated. It's just how things go. But everyone saw the video. The whole city is demanding I'm returned to service immediately. I don't have anything to worry about, Jacks. I promise. They've got county officers helping out until I return to duty."

I smiled at him. "Okay."

"I don't know what's going to happen with Marv," Jeremy said, shaking his head. "Time will tell, but the council—and a lot of Head Rock Harbor—is out for his blood. Linda's, too. You didn't hear it from me, but a few council members have implied to me that I should be preparing for a new role at the department—and be ready to interview and hire new officers."

"I don't even want to think about it right now," I said. "But, an early congratulations. You deserve it."

He reached out and put his hands on my shoulders and looked me in the eyes.

"I'm going to kind of hang around—not invade your space or anything—but keep an eye on you for the next two weeks. Is that all right?" he asked.

"I suppose I can deal with it," I teased. "Somehow I'll manage."

"I almost lost my best friend," Jeremy said with barely held back tears. "Watching over you will be my therapy."

I smiled at him, unsure what, if anything, could be said. Instead, I turned and grabbed his arm to pull it around my shoulders once more. We started walking off towards Harbor Street again. Soon the heat in town would be unbearable, the river would shrink a bit, the grass would turn brown, and the cicadas would sing another song of doom for a month. In the meantime, I was going to focus on the fact that I was going to be alive to see and hear it all.

"Why do you think he really did it?" Jeremy asked quietly. "Jealousy? I don't completely buy it."

I didn't need to think about. I knew the answer.

"Two queer guys solving all the murders and crimes lately? One of them likely to be promoted and become his boss?" I shrugged under Jeremy's arm. "Doesn't take a genius."

"I know," Jeremy sighed as we rounded the corner onto Harbor Street. "I just didn't want to admit it to myself. I thought he was actually my friend. I mean, I know he was a coworker. A fellow officer. A brother in blue. All that crap. But I thought we were *real* friends."

At the front of the shop, I turned to look at Jeremy.

"He's a bad person," I said. "It has nothing to do with you. When people let us down, it's not our fault."

"A couple visits with a shrink and you're suddenly a guru?" Jeremy reached up to boop my nose as he smiled.

I laughed, but stared at him.

"I mean it," I said. "Ashley is a piece of crap. You're a good guy, Germ. You always have been."

He stared at me, his smile growing as his cheeks reddened.

"Even when all the evidence pointed to you, I knew in my heart that it was a red herring," I said. "There's no world, no universe, no alternate reality, where someone could convince me that you'd do those kinds of things. Even when we're pretending like we aren't the best of friends forever. Take that as you will."

Jeremy stared at me for the longest time, and finally, a grin burst onto his face and he looked down at his feet. He reached up and scratched the back of his neck. The gesture, made by Jeremy, was attractive.

"So," Jeremy took a deep breath and looked at me, "is it too soon after…everything…to ask you a serious question?"

I shrugged.

"Can't get any more traumatized, I figure," I said.

We both chuckled.

"Jacks," Jeremy said slowly, "would you go out on a date with me? A real date? A special date. Where I show you how special you are to me?"

I smiled at him.

"I mean," I said coolly, "where are you taking me? Do I need to dress up? Are you paying? What are we talking about here?"

Jeremy grinned. "I was thinking that maybe we'd go up to Dubuque. See a movie or a play. Go out to dinner. Maybe some dancing. Or a walk along the river. As long as you're happy, I'll be happy."

"Sounds like you haven't put much thought into it," I said. "I don't know…"

Jeremy lifted his nose in the air haughtily.

"Well, sir, once you have come upon an answer, call upon me and—"

Reaching up, I tangled my fingers in Jeremy's golden curls and pulled his head down. Plastering my lips to his, I did my best to give him a kiss he wouldn't forget. His hands immediately went to my hips and his fingers dug into my flesh through my clothes as he returned the gesture. Dropping my arms to wrap them around his neck, I continued the kiss, letting Jeremy know that a first date was certainly in the future.

When I finally pulled away, my arms still around his neck, Jeremy was rosy-cheeked and grinning. My cheeks felt warm and I felt tingly in my belly. His fingers loosened their grip on me, but he didn't take his hands away.

"You know," I said, "a play and dinner and a walk along the river sounds perfect."

"As long as you're happy, I'm happy," Jeremy repeated.

Slowly, I let my arms slide from his neck. Jeremy begrudgingly followed my lead and his hands fell back to his sides.

I stepped away and approached the front door of the shop.

"You know," I said, turning my head to look at Jeremy, "there's something important you need to know about me."

"What's that?" He grinned at me.

"I'm not a 'do you want to come up for a coffee' on the first date kind of guy," I said. "Just so you're aware."

Jeremy nodded. "I can respect that. I still want to go on a date. And another after that. And another. As many as you'll accept."

I nodded back. We locked eyes for a moment.

"Since we're not on a first date now," I chewed at my lip, "do you want to come up for a cup of coffee?"

Jeremy grinned wickedly. "*Coffee?* Right now?"

"No. Next Tuesday in your Aunt Margaret's living room," I said. "Yes, dingus. *Coffee.* Right now."

He laughed warmly.

"Coffee sounds amazing," Jeremy said.

I crooked my head at the shop. "Come on."

Unlocking the front door, I led us into the dark shop. I grabbed Jeremy's hand and led him towards the stairs. As we passed the check-out counter, Rattlesnatches raised his head from his nap and eyed us for a moment. Taking stock of the situation, he yawned, then lowered his head back to his paws to continue his nap. If anything, Rattlesnatches is great at reading a room.

Upstairs, I led Jeremy into the apartment and shut the door behind us. Even if he could read a room, Rattlesnatches didn't necessary need access to every one of them. Not all the time. But definitely not at certain times. One of us being traumatized by the things we'd seen was enough for the time being.

*Jackson, Jeremy, Rattlesnatches, and the rest will
return in BANG BANG HE SHOT HER DOWN
(HEAD ROCK HARBOR MYSTERY #4)!*

About the Author

Chase Connor spends his days writing about the people who live (loudly and rent-free) in his head when he's not busy being enthusiastic about naps and snacks. Chase started his writing career as a confused gay teen looking for an escape from reality. Ten years later, one of the books he wrote during those years, *Just A Dumb Surfer Dude: A Gay Coming-of-Age Tale*, was published independently. Chase has numerous projects in various stages of completion lined up for publishing. Chase is a multi-genre author, but always with a healthy dollop of gay.

Chase can be reached at
chaseconnor@chaseconnor.com
On Bluesky as chaseconnorbooks
On Instagram as chaseconnorbooks
On Threads as chaseconnorbooks
He can also be found on his website www.chaseconnor.com
or on Goodreads

SIGN UP FOR THE CHASE CONNOR BOOKS NEWSLETTER AT CHASECONNOR.COM

Chase has several novellas/novels for sale in e-book, paperback, hardback, and audiobook formats wherever books are sold.